Newshounds

by

Peter J. Pritchard

Grosvenor House
Publishing Limited

The right of Peter J. Pritchard to be identified as the author of this
work has been asserted by him in accordance with Section 78
of the Copyright, Designs and Patents Act 1988

The book cover picture is copyright to Peter J. Pritchard

This book is published by
Grosvenor House Publishing Ltd
28-30 High Street, Guildford, Surrey, GU1 3EL.
www.grosvenorhousepublishing.co.uk

A CIP record for this book
is available from the British Library

ISBN 978-1-78148-335-0

GIBRALTAR

Prologue

The distinctive smell of fresh rain made a gasping effort to overcome the pervasive odour of burger buns, kebab cafés and diesel fumes that swept around Kings Cross railway station. Slumped in a tired Ford Mondeo, Special Branch Police Sergeant Albert Cosgrove lit another cigarette, took a drag and threw it in disgust, out of the window.

"£10 fine for littering, Serge," grinned his much younger partner, Bob Bevan.

"Shut the fuck up" said Cosgrove, who actually quite liked the 'fast track' graduate policeman, despite the fact that in two or three years it was quite possible he'd be his boss.

"Why do they do it Serge?" asked Bevan, peering through the murk at an equally tired Mondeo moving along the kerbside, some 100 yards ahead of them.

"Well, I've always put them into two groups. There are those who are genuine losers, alone through divorce, physically unattractive, low esteem, and pay for whatever affection and physical comfort these girls pretend to offer. The others are the genuine sex offenders who really need the raw excitement of illicit sex with underage girls, living in a state of permanent lust for schoolgirls, or boys. They aren't particularly dangerous, except if the whole bag of worms unravels and down the tubes go their careers, family and social acceptance."

"Sounds like you've made a real study of it," observed Bevan.

Cosgrove grunted and said "when I joined Special Branch twenty-five years ago, I never thought I would end up nurse-maiding our political lords and masters round the back streets of London. So much for illusions of protecting national security and all that dogs bollocks. Now who the fuck cares".

"Do you think he knows we're trailing him?" asked Bevan, offering Albert a polo mint, anything to stop him from lighting up another fag.

"You ask me," said Cosgrove, "but I doubt it. When the balls are full, the brains are empty, to quote an old one."

"But how can the Deputy Prime Minister possibly think he can escape undetected for an hour, let alone a whole night? I know Gladstone the night walker did it to 'rescue' prostitutes in Soho but in this day and age of 24 hour surveillance, this has to be nothing short of madness."

"Well, we know how he does it, the assumption is he doesn't! Home to his parliamentary flat, down in the lift to the underground car park, leaves in this scrapheap of a car he assumes we don't know about, and off to go. Having got away with it over the months, he must be confident Special Branch are happy to watch his flat all night without dicking around, to use a pun, to see if he's actually at home."

Both policemen moved awkwardly in their seats as they sat up to peer a little more closely at the scene unfolding before them. The grimy Mondeo in front of them had slowed then stopped under a lamppost. The car itself seemed to be embarrassed under the gaudy glow of the sodium lamp. Even Henry Ford himself would hardly be proud to be the manufacturer of this car. Dirty, dented and violated, like the whore it was about to pick up.

Except she wasn't. The young girl who stepped forward to the edge of the pavement was tall, slim with a model's figure, legs up to her arse and a pretty, if tired and over-made up, face.

She leant into the car, her short skirt riding up almost to reveal her buttocks. Her top dropped open to reveal a lacy bra and schoolgirls precocious breasts. It didn't take long to walk round to the passenger side of the car, slide in and...

"Would you fucking believe it," said Cosgrove "all this fucking illegality and she still puts her seatbelt on."

Following at what they imagined was a safe distance; the two Fords danced their macabre two-step around the side-streets of Camden until the first stopped outside what should have been a rather elegant Victorian townhouse. Instead, the varied selection of door bells set on a crude wooden panel beside a battered front door told their own story. Even in this light the worn facade of the building with the odd broken window and thick weeds struggling for survival on the front steps said 'welcome to our doss house'.

Parking was not a problem with many of the meter bays abandoned for the night. Even the gaps in the residents' parking permit areas intimated that this was not a des res area.

The couple left the car and scurried up the steps of the ghetto property. A fumble with the keys and they shimmied inside. The man taking a furtive glance over his shoulder expecting perhaps to see a 'Hello' magazine photographer about to capture a story that would make Fergie's topless dalliance with John Bryant or de Sanchezs' toe-sucking episode with David Mellor seem like Snow White and the Seven Dwarfs.

Soon a dim light lit up a third floor window. Even from across the street, the tatty curtains could be seen desultorily flapping as the chill night breeze funnelled between the terraced houses.

"And so to bed" intoned Cosgrove lowering the seat back with a mechanism that, like everything else in the car, had seen better days. The background chatter of the police radio stuttered nonstop with its calls for assistance, reports of foul deeds being perpetrated by the minute.

"I could do with a piss" said Bevan, unlocking another polo mint. "I can't wait until we're relieved at 7 o'clock."

Cosgrove grimaced and said "was that supposed to be some god awful smart ass joke, cos if it was, shove it."

"Serge, would I try to bamboozle you with some obscure obfuscation use of the English language?"

Deciding against a rejoinder that might backfire on himself, Cosgrove said "well, be quick. There's an alleyway round the corner but make sure the rats don't mistake your willy for a mouse."

"So tell me more Serge" said Bevan, "how does he get away with it? He's DPM, he's kerb crawling, it's underage sex, it's adultery. All we need is evidence of buggery to complete a charge sheet that would send you or I down for years. Mind you, given the opportunity

I wouldn't crawl over that little number to get to you, Serge."

"Listen you little piss-taking university scum bag, don't you ever make jokes like that again, do you hear, or I'll ram your truncheon so far up your arse, your eyes will drop out."

"Shit Serge, I didn't mean to be offensive or anything. I mean, it was a joke – or are they off duty only?"

"Okay I'm sorry too", Albert Cosgrove took a polo and nodded his thanks.

"It's just that I have a fourteen year old daughter, not dissimilar in appearance to our Miss Penelope and it's no joke. She treats her mother and me like aliens, typical teenage hypersensitivity, but always with the real threat that one day her bed will not be slept in and she's gone. Drugs, undesirable boyfriends, shop lifting, unprotected sex, you name it, it's all here my friend in deepest Hounslow.

So to your question, why is our man getting away with it, the best answer in the book – politics, control and power. We wouldn't be here if the Deputy Prime Minister's boss didn't want us here, and when he doesn't want us here then the camera in this car will be operated by a photo journalist in a much more comfortable vehicle."

"Is the back of the building under surveillance?" Bevan knew as soon as he said it, it was open house opportunity for poor quality humour.

"Worried about a rear entry?" guffawed Cosgrove, the rictus of a smile.

"The other reason the powers that be are spending good tax payers' money on our finger licking DPM, is to avoid another fiasco that pushed Alan Greene over the edge."

Cosgrove opened his triple deck sandwich and muttered a curse as a piece of tomato dropped into his lap. Bob Bevan contrived to conceal a belch as his chicken tandoori came back to remind him that pissing was the least of his problems on an all night surveillance in the back streets of London.

"Strange how novelists always seem to miss the calls of nature when they describe the tedious hours spent in dark cars parked in anonymous hostile housing estates."

"As I was saying," Cosgrove said, warming to his story, "Alan Greene was the new Attorney General and was eighteen months into his job in 1995 when his world fell apart. Like our Deputy Prime Minister, he was a regular kerb crawler in the Kings Cross area, but this night he had the misfortune to run foul of a new enthusiastic woman police officer who arrested him. Our hero, instead of pulling rank or any excuse imaginable, simple put his hands up and copped for it. The rest of the story is history. Disgrace, resignation, divorce and ultimately suicide, and into the dust bin of history for apparently a fine lawyer who promised to be the best Attorney General the country had for years."

"I thought his wife had stood by him, Serge" said Bevan, "and they went to live abroad."

"They did" affirmed Cosgrove, "and went to Menorca where they had a holiday home, but it didn't last."

"Christ, what a mess people make of their lives, it makes feeling guilty about watching porno movies fade into insignificance. "

"So here we are, trying to ensure that a similar fate doesn't happen to our boy. Of course, we'll be here only until it's politically convenient to pull the plug or whatever other fate is deemed necessary."

Six am, and thermos flasks of coffee later, the two officers viewed the departure of their man. The front door closed with barely a click as the old Yale locked itself on another night of wasted lives. Round the corner a stray dog added its steady stream of urine to the pool left by Special Branch.

Most people like to believe that senior police officers represent the best that the force can offer. Integrity, pride in the job, a determination to root out evil at whatever sacrifice and cost is necessary.

Bad news on this one.

Sir Kevin Mulhouse-Smith had risen to his present pre-eminence because of graft, not in spite of it. Amazingly he survived his spell in West End Central Vice Squad in the 60s without so much as a single glance at why he commuted every day from a detached house in Esher. His career afterwards became a blur of opportunistic arrests, brutal in-house management style and an arm lock of gratuitous seedy information on anyone brave enough to attempt to block his relentless rise up the promotional ladder. Fat, fifty and foxy summed up Londons' chief dick.

Ironically his Rambo image had made him one of the most popular MPCs in recent years. Forget the intellectual decorum of Condon and the introspective musings of Stephens, Smith's club-swinging, boot-kicking approach to street crime had won him the plaudits of every Londoner who had been raped, robbed or mugged. Smiths' philosophy was simple, 'respectable' organised criminals who thieved and conned their way into corporate fortunes were legitimate targets for civilised policing. The rest were scum. Drug peddlers, street muggers, ram raiders, pederasts, car thieves, anyone who made life inconvenient or uncomfortable for respectable folk were treated like the shit they were. It soon became clear at ground level and below, that Metropolitan Police Officers who bent the rules governing physical abuse of prisoners, tampering with evidence, and generally pissing on the shit, were protected at the highest level by a mafia style Omerta.

All this had been made clear to the Prime Minister in the earliest days of his official residence at No10.

"You keep out of my patch, and I'll keep your Deputy Prime Minister out of his political grave."

It hadn't been Smiths intention to let the Prime Minister in on his Deputy's grubby little secret, but late one evening the Prime Minister had requested to be connected to his deputy to ask a favour over handling the following days Question Time. The mansion flats receptionist, after failing to connect with the house phone, had summoned the duty Special Branch officer to take the call. It took minutes to reluctantly disclose that his bird had flown the coop.

The Prime Minister had been almost apoplectic with rage and demanded to know, what if anything, they knew of his whereabouts.

"Don't fuck with me." The harsh northern accent sharpened by anger. "I'll come over myself and you can guarantee a career standing outside No10."

The young Special Branch officer caved in, telling the Prime Minister that his understudy was on the loose in Kings Cross.

"What's he doing, fucking train spotting at this time of night?"

"I think Sir, you ought to talk to a senior officer" the Special Branch officer Michael Handsworth said.

"I do not wish to talk to another officer" the Prime Minister laid the stress on each word. "I do wish to hear the full story from you. If this is beyond your power of communication, I will summon a car right now and drive to Kings Cross and join the Deputy Prime Minister for a late night coffee and we can train spot together. Does that make it absolutely and comprehensively clear to you?"

"Yes Sir, but I don't think you should do that right now because, well, err, to put it bluntly, he's not exactly here right now."

"Well, er, to put it bluntly, where the fuck is he right now?"

"He's picked up a young lady and er, taken her home."

"I don't believe I'm hearing this" the Prime Minister said incredulously.

"Are you seriously telling me the Deputy Prime Minister absconds from his flat, legs it to Kings Cross where Special Branch follow him picking up a prostitute and watch him take her back to her place?"

"Yes Sir, that's about the basics of it".

The Prime Minister picked the stub of a cigar out of an onyx ashtray, a gift from some visiting trade union official, and snapped a cheap Bic lighter. With his free hand he pressed a command button on the internal No.10 phone. No.10 never sleeps. In the secretarial department basement bunker there are always staff on duty, ready for any sudden overnight crisis. Jenny Bond answered and heard the Prime Minister clumsily picking his receiver off the hook as he balanced the other phone and wedged it under his chin.

"Please come up here as soon as possible. Not you officer, you can answer my questions from right where you are. Presumably you do know where you are?"

The young officer knew intuitively that his dreams of a police career were being crushed as surely as the Prime Minister's cigar ash was being trodden under foot into the Axminster carpet.

"Tell me, how long has this been going on? Because thinking it through very very cursorily you understand, this must have happened before or you wouldn't have known that he had left his flat or to follow him to Kings Cross."

"Well, yes sir, but I'm new to this task force so I can't really help you with the prior history of his Kings Cross routine."

"Routine, routine! You make it sound like a regular Sunday afternoon boy scout outing. Okay, okay" the Prime Minister ground out the cigar. "So, follow your present orders, whatever they are, and" the Prime Minister allowed himself a weak smile "I do realise your balls are between the upper and nether millstones so don't give up your hopes of a career quite just yet."

Jenny Bond gently tapped on the door of the Prime Ministers top floor flat and entered with an unasked for cup of coffee.

"Bribery will get you a gong one day Jenny" said the Prime Minister, gratefully accepting the well sugared coffee.

"Right, as ever, confidentiality is top priority, but you know that, and frankly I'm glad it's your experience that's here. I'm not going to bullshit you. The Deputy Prime Minister has gone walkabout with a prostitute in Kings Cross and Special Branch have seemingly kept it up their sleeve for some time. I would like you to ferret out the Met Police Commissioner and unless he's dead or abroad, get him here now. And also ask Harris, my own Special Branch Officer to come to No10 through the garden gate."

"Please sit Commissioner, I'll have coffee sent in but for the moment I will exercise the luxury of telling you in unparliamentary word speak that you have exercised fucking personal censorship over information that in itself could threaten national security if it ever really got into the wrong hands. And in your fucking hands, that could already be wrong hands."

"I don't have to listen to this," the Met chief stood and started for the door. "If you think the Deputy Prime Minister's case is unique, you have to be more naïve than I would have given you credit for."

"Sexual pervs are the rule rather than the exception in political parties. Special Branch keeps them out of trouble by trying to ensure no-one else gets near them or if they do, we have 'ways' to edit out the potential damage. Do you really want to know about the sexual proclivities of all of your political chums, cos if you do, we'll be here for a week."

The two men glared at each other, knowing that there were going to be no winners in this locking of horns.

"Anyway, don't play holier than thou with me Prime Minister, we're both compromised up to our balls if ever this leaks out because I don't imagine for one moment you're about to go public with the juiciest bit of blackmail you've probably ever got your grubby hands on in your devious political life."

It lasted for a moment, a relationship hanging in the balance, then the Prime Minister guffawed loudly.

"Christ, Kevin, if the public only knew what 'chancers' they've got leading the country's Parliament and largest police force, they'd go ape shit."

"So why the midnight summons? We could have sorted this out in the morning and all had a good nights sleep."

"More easily said than done" muttered the Prime Minister. "How many of your ground troops know about this because presumably it's been going on for a while. And, while we're at it, is there any other little bombshell lurking in the bushes I ought to know about?"

"Six months, once a month, to our definite knowledge" the Commissioner admitted "other than that, no hard evidence, but difficult to believe that he's suddenly discovered illicit sex at 55, but I suppose it's possible. As to question two, you definitely are going to gag on this one. He only picks up girls of 13 and 14. Maybe he feels safer that the chances of a teenie recognising a leading politico are pretty remote but personally I think not. These youngsters may be tarty but they are always very attractive and definitely very sexy. It is young sex he's after and sucks to anonymity."

"Hmm, see what you mean," the Prime Minister shifted through a file of ill-lit but clear enough photos. "I suppose the expression dirty, rotten, lucky bastard flits through the mind," grinned the Prime Minister, gazing at a particularly erotic youngster massaging herself into the Mondeo.

"Anyway, the sixty-four thousand dollar question is, and this is why I didn't want to wait until the morning, now that I do know about it and since the minders probably think the shit's about to hit the fan anyway, what's the chances of someone running to Max Clifford and blowing the story for thousands – presumably complete with photographic evidence?"

Before he could reply, the internal phone buzzed and Jenny announced that John Harris had arrived and was waiting in the staff kitchen.

"Let's both ask John Harris the same question because he is one of the guys on the ground and I think he does have some degree of loyalty to me, difficult though that may be to believe."

John Harris was everyone's picture of how Special Branch officers should look, Nondescript, a Marks and Spencers, middle class, mediocre, unnoticeable man, But, and no buts about it, very bright, very enthusiastic and actually well paid for his efforts.

"Good morning Sir. Good morning Prime Minister."

The Prime Minister swallowed a retort, Shouldn't 'good morning Prime Minister' come first? Maybe not, the Commissioner will still be his boss after I've written my political epitaph. The Prime Minister shook himself to stifle such irrelevant thoughts.

"Look John" said the Prime Minister, "we all three in this room now have a fairly detailed picture of the Deputy Prime Minister's philandering. No need to tell you what a time bomb this could be. Two questions, do you have any information that may be buried in your reports about the girls of their pimps or (their pimps) whatever, that could blow the lid off this? And secondly, what are the chances now that I know, that one of your people may be tempted to freelance the story to the press?"

"Simple answer, Sir, firstly we have not, as a matter of policy, attempted any post-coital surveillance if I may use the expression, on any of the girls. One, we don't particularly have the manpower, but more importantly there is no point in letting slip, however remote the possibility, that there is anything special about their 'John'. Secondly, very little risk indeed in my opinion. Special Branch officers have seen more of life's soiled underwear than you would care to believe. Maybe a Deputy Prime Minister and underage sex is juicier than the average, but that's all it is. There is frankly no evidence of physical abuse or any coercion, so quote the old two Ronnies saying, 'it's good luck to him and good luck to her'."

"Okay gentlemen, we'll leave it at that. Thank you John, I'll see you tomorrow and sorry to drag you in like this. Kevin, a final word."

The Prime Minister opened the cocktail cabinet and waved his hand at the bottles.

"You have a driver I trust, Kevin, wouldn't do to have two of my senior advisers bagged in one night."

"Make it a very large Scotch and I'll forgive the earlier insults." Sir Kevin lit a cigar offered by the Prime Minister and observed "I suppose Henry, one of these days this information will come in useful, though it's hard to imagine how extreme the circumstances will need to be, assuming of course, we're allowed the luxury of containing it within these walls. Wouldn't you be better off simply throwing him to the wolves now? It is not as if you like the man, and an involuntary disclosure of this story might do you more damage by association than you'd like, especially if it happens in two years, near the general election, when everyone is especially looking for muck to throw."

Henry Padgett Grimes cracked his left knuckle and blew a thick cloud of smoke towards the table lamp and watched it spiral upwards through the top of the shade. Smoke and hot air: the ingredients of tabloid journalism.

"No Kevin, I'm going to take the chance that we can sit on it. My cabinet is heavily divided and there is a cabal led by the Deputy, who thinks incidentally, that I don't know, who would force me out given the faintest of excuses. One day, I will nail the bastard but politically, now is not the time. When it is, our little toe rag will know what being screwed is really all about."

Gibraltar

A Novel

The time is the present and financial and social dysfunction is affecting every country in Europe. Riots have occurred in Greece, France and the UK. But no country is worse affected than Spain where 20%+ unemployment (45% under 30s) has brought thousands out onto the streets of Madrid.

The Government is paralysed by indecision until yet another general election brings in a relatively young unknown politician as Prime Minister.

Knowing that there is no quick fix to the Spanish economic problem he is determined to divert the populations aggravation into a wave of nationalistic jingoism.

The threat of civil unrest provides perfect cover to mobilise the armed forces and it is easy to find an excuse to build up military strongholds around critical national facilities such as oil refineries and harbours. One of the biggest of these is La Linea, a town dominated by a huge refinery, along the coast from Gibraltar.

Presented with this doomsday scenario of Spain sinking into chaos, the Spanish Cabinet is overwhelmed by the strategy unfolded before them. Not one of them perceives that the Prime Ministers plan is driven by a pathological hatred of the British, as much as a diversionary attention getter for the Spanish people.

Few people/voters in any country really know much or care less about the early background of their leaders until they are caught one day with their pants down or steal the crown jewels.

Focused on their own problems at home the British government is quite sympathetic to the Spanish predicament and pays little attention to the military build up around La Linea. Equally the border police, where the crossing from the mainland to Gibraltar is located, simply fail to notice the number of cars and small commercial vehicles that drive into Gibraltar to shop (tax free) carrying a family in, but no husband on return.

Similarly, Gibraltar's main yachting marinas are host to a refreshing number of Spanish yachts and motor boats bringing in welcome trade to the restaurants, bars and shops that have been affected by the fall in tourist trade as a result of the recession. Even a Spanish cruise ship ties up for a two day call.

It is that time in the early hours of the morning when the last carousers have gone wearily to bed, but before the first workers set off wearily to work, that the streets of Gibraltar come alive with people purposefully heading to the government offices and guarded entrances to the Royal Naval dockyard. Without a shot being fired or a phone call made, the frontier police are taken into custody and a column of military vehicles swarm across the causeway. Within an hour the Spanish flag is flying over the island's government buildings and Spain wakes up to the realization that Gibraltar, the insult to their sovereignty that has bugged them since it was given to the British in the Treaty of Utrecht in 1713 is once again theirs.

If the fall of the Falklands was a shock to the British, the news (when it finally sank in) was catatonic. At 6am when the information was fed to the Prime Minister sheer disbelief paralysed any sort of response for at least another hour. News that the British Ambassador in Madrid was on his way home after being unceremoniously booted out of his residency confirmed that this was no joke. Effectively as he told the nation on television, Britain is now at war with Spain.

As each hour passed, the military stranglehold on Gibraltar escalates rapidly as the Spanish navy position boats around the peninsula and the army secure every aspect of the 'islands' policing. The local civil service is given a simple option, stay at work or leave. Most choose to stay. Very soon the Spanish government confirmed that the special financial tax haven status of Gibraltar would remain. However, the airport runway across which the road into Gibraltar runs, would remain closed until further notice.

As partying continued unabated across Spain few bothered to note the British Foreign Office advising expat homeowners to lock up and leave, and holiday tour companies canceling flights and hotel reservations. It did become clear in Spain and the UK that it was not safe to be overtly Spanish or English. Tapas bars and restaurants in London and elsewhere were attacked, fire bombed and looted. Retaliation in Spain was quick to follow with expat residences and marina based boats being openly vandalised without any response from the Guardia Civil or local police.

Finally, COBRA met in London and each member in turn gave his assessment of the situation and the likely success of either military or political manoeuvres to resolve the crisis.

It became very obvious that calls from Nato, the United Nations and the EC Parliament in Strasburg, for the Spanish to respect International Treaties and withdraw were falling on very deaf ears. Not that the Spanish could hear very much over the continuing celebrations.

It is simply impractical, said the Chief of Staff to the COBRA committee, to invade Gibraltar as we did the Falklands. The loss of life would be enormous and the certainty of success equally doubtful.

Politically, the Foreign Secretary said the almost unbelievably hostile attitude of the Spanish Prime Minister to any form of dialogue ruled out the chance of a negotiated political settlement.

The British Prime Minister concluded the meeting by saying that the Spanish could enjoy their moment of glory, even though Spanish tomato growers would soon feel the pinch as a result of the UK ban on the import of any Spanish products, but we weren't beaten yet. His one and only conversation with the Spanish Prime Minister was so one-sidedly acrimonious that the conclusion had to be that desperate times would perforce require desperate measures. The next meeting would be a forum to air these.

Disliked by the British establishment, distrusted by the city and generally felt to be a 'bad egg' the owner of one of the worlds largest media groups, Media Worldwide

Corporation was in London and thoroughly enjoying the discomfiture of the British Government. He told the Managing Editors of his leading tabloid newspaper and 'Cloud' TV news channel that there must be an angle to this story that everyone had missed. Especially, how could the Spanish believe that with their economy in tatters, how could they remotely realistically believe that pissing off probably their largest European customer would help matters improve?

"It seems to me that this desperate throw of the dice to detract the Spanish voters' attention away from reality is more to do with the Spanish Prime Ministers' anti-British hatred, bordering on paranoia, than rational argument. What do we really know about him? Very little is known of his life before he came into politics and this may be the secret that we can unlock. Who do we have as correspondent in Spain?"

"Bit of a sad story there," replied the managing editor. "Young chap, fluent Spanish, married a beautiful Spanish girl, produced two delightful babies and gave us great copy from Madrid. That was until his wife and family were killed in a road accident caused by a drunken Romanian truck driver who smashed her car off a bridge into a ravine and left him bereft. He is still in Madrid and occasionally sends us in a good piece, otherwise he seems intent on drinking himself to death. No one here, frankly, has had the heart to fire him, so he is still on the books."

"Send a minder to straighten him out, who will brook no nonsense, until he has researched this story, and then it may be time to let him go."

"Well my dear," said the managing editor to the attractive but spikey blonde 25 year old something, "this is your big break. Madrid, expenses and a chance to cover yourself in glory."

In the journalists world it doesn't take long to find a newspaper reporter. There are restaurants and bars, especially bars, where the scribes, hacks, call them what you will, meet to swap stories and drink on their expenses to excess and beyond.

He was there, inebriated but not yet quite drunk. Reluctantly knowing that his paymaster had finally tracked him down, and was expecting something for his money, allowed himself to be led back to his apartment. Months of neglect had turned it into a pit but two hours of solid grafting made it reasonably habitable so that she was able to tell him that she was sleeping in the spare bedroom and more drinking was off limits.

Twelve o'clock and the crash of a wine bottle being pulled off a shelf by the front door, attached to the handle by a length of cotton made it clear that minding was a serious business and not to be messed with.

In summary, the research project started well. The records of births, marriages and deaths yielded a date some forty years before in a hospital in central Spain. But further inquiries produced very little meat until the emerging political career some ten years ago.

They hired a car and traveled into the barren, unpicturesque, mountainous centre of Spain. The hospital records kept since Franco's iron rule were, after a little financial persuasion, made available to them only to find a name, a date of birth and a village of origin. They were told that if it still existed it was kilometres away in some of the most brutal countryside in Spain.

It is hard to feel personable when you are in a small car – hot, sweaty, sleeping badly and not permitted to drink.

Nevertheless as each kilometre passed the two journalists gradually found a companionable respect for each other and for the first time he was able to share some of the emotional cataclysm that had ruined his life.

Finally they arrived in a hamlet – you couldn't call it a village, that was a throwback of 200 years or more. Walking into the tiny bar that also served as a shop, conversation died as the few old locals looked at the pair as if they had just arrived from the planet Zog.

It soon became clear that news of the momentous events in Gibraltar had not arrived in this remote wilderness. Even if it had it is doubtful if the locals would understand it.

After standing a few rounds gentle questioning finally elicited the information that the only person left who might help them was the local priest who was now they said, nearer a 100 than 80, and could be found in his tiny cell attached to the Church.

Frail, wizened but clear eyed, the priest was not going to be flannelled by a made up reason for their visit and he was told that they were researching the background of a man who was now the most important politician in Spain.

In this part of the world we depend on God not politics for our survival, said the priest, but I will tell you what I know, and it is a sad and pitiful tale.

"In the years after the second world war finished, General Franco's rule brought a surge of economic progress to Spain. The South Coast especially saw massive investment in hotels, housing and more. Poor villages like this one, with few prospects saw the youngsters leave in droves for the money and bright lights of the coast.

Maria Sanchez was no exception. At the age of 17 she fled the misery of life with her draconian parents and managed to reach the fast growing resort of Benidorm. Already it was becoming the Blackpool of Spain for British tourists, attracted by an exciting new culture and fantastically cheap booze. It was not difficult for an attractive teenager to find work in the many hotels springing up in the town.

Life was good. Sharing a small apartment with a few other hotel girls, even on a low salary was brilliant. Although it was forbidden, most of the girls had dates with young English tourists who had money and were out for a good time.

This particular evening her date was a good looking rugby playing Brit, part of a group, determined to find out if Spanish girls were really as sexy as it was believed back home. It went disastrously wrong. He got drunk and instead of a romantic end to the evening, raped her on the beach behind his hotel.

Two missed periods later and a thickening waistline told its own story. Remember this was still very Catholic Spain under a dictator whose moral code often led to the Guardia Civil ejecting tourists from the beach for being improperly (scantily) dressed.

There were no refuges, no charities and no sympathy, so the only remedy was to return home and beg her parents protection. To no avail, her parents were at once mortified, outraged, fearing social ostracism, tarred with the humiliation of a whoring daughter and a bastard child."

The old priest stopped to gather his thoughts and then continued slowly.

"She came to me for help. I was helpless, torn between the responsibilities of upholding the moral standards of the Church and this wretched girl. In the end I found an old couple, childless and living on the edge of the village to take her in. The baby was born, but nothing got better. She was shunned by the community and found living with the old couple increasingly claustrophobic and depressingly dependent on their charity. They didn't, of course, mind because the baby became the centre of their lives. That is, of course, until the young girl committed suicide and they were forced to legally adopt the baby, and hence the problem of understanding how the Prime Minister of Spain's name is at odds with the records.

Then they died of old age, and having gleaned something of the torment of his mothers life, he went into an orphanage run by an order of nuns who made it quite clear that as a bastard he would be treated like one. His hatred of his father for abandoning his mother resulting in her misery and suicide was fuelled by the treatment meted out to him. I think I have the original birth certificate in the Church if you are interested."

Lifting the ancient tome down the priest turned the yellowing parchment pages until the faded entry of forty years ago was found.

Peering over his shoulder the two journalists puzzled for a moment at their flicker of recognition of the fathers name.

Then the staggering truth hit them.

It was the name of the present BRITISH PRIME MINISTER!

"It all fits doesn't it?"

The media tycoon was beside himself with glee. "Son hates father and goes bananas to get his own back. The $64,000 question is, what do we do with the story? It's a scoop beyond imagination but should we tell our revered leader first and risk a D Notice or simply publish and be damned. I could do with a little government backing to my purchase of Rattle Media Group and less interference from the Monopolies Commission."

The accountants in the group saw a clear financial advantage in going down this route. The journalists however were howling for blood with one of the tastiest revelations on their hands for a long time.

The Media King called the two journalists into his office to celebrate with a bottle of champagne and was amazed to be turned down in favour of fruit juice cocktails. Clearly the Spanish sun wasn't just only for ripening oranges!

Their disappointment at the possibility of the story being 'spiked' only added to the owners personal angst with the way the British political system treated him, so after a few more reassuring nods from the Companies lawyers the decision was made to publish and to hell with the consequences.

The same day the story broke COBRA convened again. But before any discussion resumed about Gibraltar itself, the position of the Prime Minister himself came under scrutiny. The Deputy Prime Minister led the charge that the PM's position was now untenable either with the British public or the International media and political circles. How could there be any satisfactory dialogue between a bastard son and his delinquent father.

The Deputy Prime Minister made it clear that he was ready to step up if the PM stepped down. An opportunist move to seize what the Deputy Prime Minister had rightly believed to be his for years.

It was a revolt that was to be crushed as quickly as it began. The PM asked for a temporary adjournment of the meeting and requested the Deputy Prime Minister to stay behind.

"I never thought the day would come when your disloyalty would be so evident, but fearing that you may be plotting such a move I have brought some Special Branch pictures taken over the years of your keen interest in the welfare of very young girls around the Kings Cross area of London."

"Quite so PM," said the Deputy Prime Minister, "unless you want my resignation now, I suggest we reconvene and pretend I never spoke."

No one quite understood the nature of the changed demeanour of the Deputy Prime Minister but in any case the PM's doomsday analysis of the options open to them closed their minds to anything else.

In essence, he said, since the last meeting the Spanish have seized control of Gibraltar so that any military intervention by land, sea or air was out of the question.

Regardless of the latest disclosure of his relationship with the Spanish Prime Minister, diplomacy seemed doomed to failure before it could get off the ground.

Therefore option three was the only one left. By the time the PM finished the meeting was reeling as a combination of incredulity, doubts about the Prime Minister's sanity and a prolonged buzz of 'let's go for it'.

Although the army and air force had been stood down, the Royal Navy was still in position at a distance from the Rock. The aircraft carrier sent the occasional reconnaissance aircraft over the peninsula, and submarines shadowed the few Spanish diesel electric submarines they still had in service, and which were completely outclassed by the Trafalgar nuclear submarines of the Royal Navy.

In Madrid the reaction to the UK news revelation brought a sobering winding down of the euphoric partying. As with many truths in life, nothing is ever as it seems, and the Spanish thinking classes began wondering whether they hadn't been betrayed by a giant con trick to satisfy one mans ego. However, the general feeling was 'in for a centime, in for a euro' and lets stay on the roller coaster for the ride.

And the ride was about to begin in earnest. Aboard aircraft carrier HMS Illustrious the Prime Minister addressed the senior officers and the two commanders of the Trafalgar class submarine's SSN Torbay and Trenchant.

The Spanish are guilty of international piracy and it is your job to bring them to justice by persuading them to hand back Gibraltar to its rightful owners, the Gibraltarians.

You will in five days time fire a cruise missile with a conventional warhead to a rather deserted valley outside the tiny village of Castillblanco where the Spanish Prime

Minister was brought up. This is unless they respond to our ultimatum to leave Gibraltar within five days. If this doesn't focus their attention sufficiently ten days later two cruise missiles will destroy a more significant target. It will be hoped by now the Spanish will be taking us seriously and vacating Gibraltar as fast as they can.

However, if they persist they will be warned that within another twenty-one days an ICBM with a nuclear warhead will destroy the town of Ciudad Real, hopefully with the residents having been evacuated by the authorities.

Let no-one be in any doubt that this is a war they started and we are determined to win. If they should attempt reprisals against the Gibraltarians our subs will retaliate. We could fight a prolonged sea war, sinking ships and blockading port, but as swiftly as they invaded Gibraltar they must leave.

Or has the Prime Minister taken leave of his senses?

The first diplomatic note was delivered on Friday, with a scrolling down date of five days from Monday. It was not expected the Spanish would take it seriously and they didn't. Consequently on Saturday with a loud rushing sound, Castillblanco became even less attractive, and home to even less sheep than before.

It is difficult to imagine the shock and horror that swept news of this act around Europe and the World.

Opinions ranged from outright condemnation to a grudging admiration for such decisive action.

There was no immediate response from Madrid and, apart from predictable tut tutting from Strasbourg and the United Nations, no-one seemed able to formulate a reasoned punishment for this act of vandalism.

The second 'call my bluff' challenge was issued by the PM personally when he managed, by some mistake of the Spanish PM's office telephone receptionist, to speak personally to him before being cut off.

So a second diplomatic note was delivered but this time it was also circulated to the media as it was felt this would provide a stark warning to the locals to abandon the area. A valley in the Sierra de Segura mountains, close to the more famous Sierra Nevada ranges was felt to provide a sufficiently dramatic backdrop without causing too much disruption for the local inhabitants.

"Sadly, I have to report to the House that our game plan is not working. Spain has not been persuaded to come to the negotiating table or accept any form of mediation, so unless we back down, it is time to up the stakes. Before doing so however, I will make one final attempt to meet and reason with my son."

A curt refusal from Madrid put paid to this idea, so the countdown began.

A much bigger bang than the first resounded around the villages high in the Sierra de Segura mountains ten days later, but with greater collateral damage to buildings and roads. Loss of life was minimal, but the UK was still demonised by the media as a nation of barbarians.

As the Royal Navy's nuclear submarines patrolled off the Southern Spanish coast, it became increasingly obvious that the shortest straw option was going to be unavoidable unless the UK faced a humiliating climb down. Indeed could anyone ask a Royal Navy submarine commander to fire a nuclear bomb at a target which might contain thousands of citizens (unwilling to believe that such a fate could befall them at a time when most people still regarded post war euro nations at peace with one another). Surely the UK couldn't <u>nuke</u> Spain!

Unthinkable! Or, what if?

Of course at the heart of the problem, no-one bothered to ask the Gibraltarians how they felt about politicians threatening to nuke people on their behalf. Under the Spanish, life as it always does, carried on as normal apart from the fact that the majority of British pubs in Gibraltar started selling more San Miguel and Estrella beer rather than John Smiths.

'Cloud' TV attempted to send the two journalists who had been so successful in locating the Spanish Prime Minister's heritage into Gibraltar but they were refused entry along with other journalists.

In Spain, as in the UK, the public were still in a state of shock that this spat over the fate of such an insignificant, and if you've been there, hideous, rock could be causing so much trouble.

The day that the UK government announced the third ultimatum, many peace protestors took to the streets saying that no national pride could be worth the risk of so much bloodshed and devastation. There were quite a lot of protestors in the streets of Cuidad Real as well when they discovered they were the target of the threat.

Deep in the heart of the designated Trafalgar class nuclear submarine the Commander too debated whether to resign his commission rather than go to his grave agonising over the deaths of thousands of innocent civilians on his conscience. But just as wartime leaders killed millions, if you join up and take the queen's shilling, you cannot walk away if orders do not suit you. So yes, he would stay and press the button.

So as the countdown began, diplomatic pressure for a negotiated settlement reached new levels. But it is difficult to reach any compromise when neither side really believes the threat is real (Spain) or would be necessary (UK).

However, as tension rose the Spanish government did start to make plans to evacuate the city. Already there was a steady stream of people in cars, on foot, catching trains and buses, moving away from the town they were now calling Ciudad Unreal, many heading towards Madrid, only some 200 kilometres north.

At last frustration in Gibraltar broke out as locals took to the streets complaining of Guardia Civil harassment and increasing interference by Madrid imposing many new taxes, especially the Spanish equivalent to VAT (IVA) at 18%. Riot police, the Guardia and army retaliated with batons, tear gas and water cannon soon dispersing the crowds, but encouraging a new wave of Pro-British support for the hard line policy being followed in London.

Nato and the UN offered to take over Gibraltar with peace-keeping forces, but along with suggestions of a referendum or a long term lease back, each idea fell by the wayside. There were even wild rumours that the Spanish intended to invade the Scilly Isles or the Isle of Wight, but in the event it was recognised the Spanish Navy was no match for the UK's navy spearheaded by six Trafalgar class nuclear submarines.

With only five days to go the world began to hold its breath as neither side made any move to compromise, or back down. In Madrid, Parliament was in permanent session, because not everyone thought Gibraltar was worth the effort, particularly as unemployment in the past weeks had rocketed past 25% as the holiday industry laid off myriads of workers. Who wants to go on holiday to a country under imminent threat of a nuclear attack.

In London, secretly the British Prime Minister conceded that possibly a nuclear strike was a bit over the top and a raid by a quantity of cruise missiles would be sufficient, but he would make the decision at the last moment. In the meantime, let the bastards sweat.

Two days to go and the Spanish Prime Minister went on television in a nationwide broadcast to say that he took full responsibility for the present crisis, but his personal fight did not cloud his belief that Gibraltar belonged to Spain. To demonstrate his determination and solidarity with the Spanish people he would personally travel to Ciudad Real and stay there with the sick, infirm, poor and those too old to travel until either he died with them or proved the British threat was a hollow drum.

That evening Turbulent landed off the South Coast of Spain, six of Hereford's finest. In the old days the black rubber dinghy would have been punctured and sunk by the SAS but new rules on saving tax payers money meant the young naval subby turned it round and the electric outboard silently returned it to mother.

The stained white van with orange warning roof lights was where it should be and was parked by dawn outside the perimeter road alongside the Spanish airbase from where the Prime Minster would depart after an emotional and highly publicised PR event. The new European Austa AWIOI helicopter on loan for trials with the

Spanish forces would take less than two hours to take him to the centre of Ciudad Real.

They set up their 'road works' barriers and signs and went to work like any other lookalike Spanish navvies. Two of them spoke Spanish fluently and explained to a passing security patrol there was a reported water leak and they would only be there for a day or so. It is amazing that if you look like a duck, talk like a duck and walk like a duck, people think you are a duck. Putting the SAS up against sloppy, lazy and inefficient Spanish security was like taking candy from a baby and after only a few hours they were split up and homeward bound.

After a highly charged speech and tearful farewells to his wife, actually stage managed as they would soon be divorced, he climbed aboard. Watched by millions, the helicopter rose swiftly and appeared to jig its nose in salute before exploding in a ball of flame so fierce that there was hardly anything left to fall to the ground.

The Spanish Cabinet under its acting Prime Minister was unanimous that the game was up. No one could ever prove it was the Brits who sabotaged the plane, and if it was, who could really blame them for not wanting a martyred Prime Minister when Ciudad Real went up in smoke.

An immediate message was sent to London simply stating that in national mourning the Spanish would withdraw from Gibraltar within 24 hours and would the British government consider new talks regarding the future of Gibraltar.

Although knowing it would be pretty meaningless, the Foreign Secretary sympathised with the death of their Prime minister, welcomed the release of Gibraltar and as a magnanimous gesture said of course talks would be scheduled as soon as possible.

In the midst of an overflowing of national pride and alcohol, few people around him saw a very haggard Prime Minister not perhaps getting into the swing of things as would be expected. It is very difficult to celebrate knowing that you gave the order to murder your only child.

They discovered him the following morning face down on his desk with a single gunshot wound to his head, a simple message written on a pad:

In memory of my son.

The End

The End

THE
ARABIAN
PRINCESS

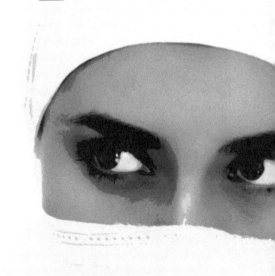

Prologue

"In the name of Allah, most compassionate, most merciful"

"Pregnancy due to illegitimate sexual intercourse is no excuse for carrying out an abortion. Islam condemns and rejects illicit sex and everything that leads to it". Allah most high says

"And do not even come close to adultery, for it is a shameful deed and an evil".
(Surah al-Isra v:32)

Islam has also laid down a legal punishment (hadd) for the one who is guilty of this grievous crime.

"Then came to the Messenger of Allah a woman from Ghamid, and said "Oh Messenger of Allah, I have committed adultery so purify me." He turned her away. On the following day she said "O Messenger of Allah, why do you turn me away. Perhaps you turn me away as you turn away Ma'iz. By Allah, I have become pregnant".
He said "Well if you insist upon it, then go away until you give birth."

When she delivered she came to the Messenger of Allah with the child wrapped in a piece of cloth and said "Here is the child I have given birth to."

He said "Go away and suckle him until you wean him."

When she had weaned him she came to him with the child who was holding a piece of bread in his hand and said "Oh prophet of Allah! Here is the child as I have weaned him and he eats food."

The Messenger of Allah entrusted the child to one of the Muslims and then pronounced punishment. And she was put in a ditch up to her chest and he commanded the people and they stoned her.

Then the Messenger of Allah (Allah bless him and give him peace) gave the order regarding her, hence he prayed over her and she was buried.

"Wow!" As a journalist recently sent to cover the Middle East you really have to hand it to these guys, they certainly know how to treat women!

Since coming to live in Riyadh as correspondent for the Telegraph newspaper, my perceptions, conceptions and misconceptions regarding Allah, Muslims and the Islamic faith swing widely according to which fundamentalists or modern secularists I am listening to. One thing is certain, in Saudi Arabia, home of Walhabi Islam, Abdulaziz Ibn in the early 20th century restored the Saudi Kingdom and melded political and religious ideologies into the official creed for state and society.

Is this so boring? I hope not because this puritanical version of Islam spawned the Taliban and Osama Bin Laden. It still rules Saudi Arabia and although many

Arabs seem to regard camel shagging and young boys as fair game woe betide an illegitimate pregnancy. Even more so if the victim is a white, non-Muslim. Plenty have been seduced by wealthy young Saudis coming to the UK full of sweet talk, sweet bodies, amazing cars and shed-fulls of cash only to find that once pregnant, the lads disappear like the shifting sands of the desert from whence they came.

Be warned! A western woman who gives birth out of wedlock is unlikely to be accepted by a Saudi family.

Chapter 1

From the moment I could run and think I knew I was going to be a journalist. I was the earliest to read and write in my infants' school and confounded adults by an almost perfect photographic memory, especially for faces.

By the time I was 10 I was penning short stories and infuriating teachers by reminding them of unkept promises, "But you said....last week...that..."

Perhaps my moment of greatest juvenile precocity came during the local village cricket derby. My father, an archetypal middle class, middle ranking civil servant, lived and breathed our cricket club. But this year the game with our neighbouring village had more edge to it than a razor blade. Rivalry between the two sides had always been fierce, but last year sex gave a special twist to "bowling a maiden over".

Behind the club during afternoon tea one of their team was found bonking one of our teams' girlfriends. Word spread to the bar and a wit (not my father) added fuel to an already explosive atmosphere by commenting that this was the best example of "legs before wicket" he had witnessed.

Two broken noses, two broken chairs and two broken hearts later, order was restored by our local Mr Plod.

So this year you could feel the electricity in the air. So in steps yours truly and says to my father "that chap with the grey hair and cravat in their side, wasn't he in the English cricket team a few years back?"

An unwritten rule of our local derby was that players were amateurs and lived in the respective villages. Father who for all his faults had every respect for my memory took the score card into the club office and googled his name. Not only was I bang on that he had had an albeit short-lived career as an English batsman, but he lived in Surrey.

My father who had perfected the "I say old chap, this is not cricket" turn of phrase, forced the opponents to stand him down. One can never know but they lost by only a few runs and I was the hero of the day.

When I was seventeen and star pupil at our local independent college, my father cleared his throat and in Churchillian tones announced it was time to talk about choice of university.

"Ah" said I, "now you mention it dad, I have been intending to talk to you about my future as actually I am not going."

"Not going to university?"

I couldn't quite fathom whether this was a question or simply an expression of incredulity.

"So what are you going to do, join the army, take articles, become a monk or a career, as is most popular these days, a DSS drop out?"

"Well actually Dad, I am starting my new job at the end of the summer term as a dispatch clerk with the Surrey Comet."

Apoplectic apoplexy, a Vesuvius eruption, a tsunami, nothing quite captures adequately the next few moments. But after the storm came the deadly calm.

"I hope," said father "that your salary will pay the rent for your new home because it certainly won't be here. And your sister will be seventeen next year so your car that I funded can be left here for her to drive."

Hell has no fury like a father's ambition for his son, scorned.

Oops, hadn't figured on the car retaliation bit, still after the 2012 Olympics cycling is the new Brit status symbol. Only hope I can afford even a second hand Raleigh. Newspaper remuneration is not especially rewarding especially at despatch clerk level.

Despite the tears and protestations of my mother, father was 'like' unmoved. "Never darken these doors again" – whilst not actually said, was written all over his body language.

So I left home and toiled in the depths of the Surrey Comet. Father simply could not countenance the simple idea that I knew that to be a journalist you did not start at the top and work your way down. Just the thought of being in a building housing even a local rag excited me more than I could say. But the lesson learned from this experience is perhaps the bedrock of all journalism; never trust anyone because a suspicious mind is at the heart of finding a good story.

So if that was lesson one, lesson two of behaving like a complete shit came a few years later.

Richard Goodfellow the Managing Editor was, and still is, one of the most likeable, generous and even handed men I have ever met. He even looked like a journalist should, grey curly hair, slightly built and with a dress style that combined Dr Who with Wurzel Gummidge.

After despatching despatches for two years, my patience was finally rewarded with an assignment to cover a WVS meeting. Richard, bless him, had never forgotten my final interview, and burning ambition to become a journalist.

By the time I was 21 I was receiving regular jobs to cover for absent reporters. The greatest day came when I was given my press card. Now I was a real journalist, and soon to be shit.

Although it was only a local rag the Comet was actually quite influential. It covered a large part of Surrey, and was courted by everyone from local MP's looking for praise from the local hoi polloi, to the police claiming that the same hoi polloi didn't understand them.

So on this day Richard was off on a junket with local business bigwigs and asked me if I wouldn't mind accompanying his wife to another shindig where the Comet was expected to show a leg. I expect by now you are already one step ahead of where this is going. And you're right.

Lynn turned out to be bright, beautiful, articulate and much younger than I had expected. We got on like a house on fire. Lunch turned into dinner. My thoughts of what it would be like to get into her knicks, after a few more drinks, became hers as well.

And so to bed.

At least there were no children to add to guilt. Two years passed of wonderful secretive, illicit, innovative sex. But I knew in my darkest place that Lynn was always hurting for Richard, the innocent cuckold. And in those post-coital moments, I knew too that he did not deserve our disloyalty.

Perhaps the morning that he called me into his office I sensed before I even sat down that this was going to be the Armageddon that the guilt, which nagged me constantly, had arrived. My role at the paper, with Richards guidance and tutelage, had reached a seniority way beyond my years and experience and now it was to receive its comeuppance.

"Gareth, your position at the paper is frankly about to become redundant."

Bullshit! I was the most successful journalist the paper had ever had and he knew it.

"For me personally it will be a source of loss that you will be leaving us and I know that my wife will feel the same."

Ouch! Worse to come:

"You have been a source of pride to me as your talents have expanded and a real friend to the family. But you have outgrown us here at the Comet, and it's time to move on."

For God's sake Richard get on with it, get the knife out and plunge into my duplicitous back.

"I have a long and dear friend at the Telegraph who recently over lunch expressed his frustration with the standard of journalists that even his paper was recruiting. There was no doubt in my mind that I knew how to fill that gap. I told him for personal reasons you will have to trust me, but by all means send someone in confidence to check out my references."

"You may remember, Gareth, a day and night spent with the lovely Chrissie Noakes. Well, thanks to her undercover and underclothed experiences with you, you start work on Monday as a fully accredited journalist with the Daily Telegraph. Congratulations now get out and clear your desk!"

You incredible, unbelievable, sensational bastard! When God created you, you broke the mould. If this is the price of adultery, heaven knows what the cost of marriage must be.

It wasn't until much later that I obtained some record of that evening when Richard returned home. Lynn, solid as ever, was preparing dinner when he came in looking somewhat distracted but unusually assertive. He insisted on opening a fresh bottle of their better white wine, left a bottle of red to breathe and lit table candles.

Lynn, unsure where this was heading asked whether they were celebrating anything special that wasn't in her diary.

"You could say so" said Richard "But let's enjoy dinner first. If I may say, you look really lovely tonight and I am sorry that as a husband I probably haven't been everything you would have wanted in bed and out of it."

By now Lynn was finding it difficult to breathe.

He knows! He knows! Oh God, he knows!

"Excellent dinner and now for the good news. Gareth's position at the Comet has for some time been increasingly untenable and today I finally decided that enough was enough and said he should leave."

Lynn sat and stared at Richard, trying to read something, anything, in his expression.

"Oh I see" was the best she could manage.

"When does he go?"

"Go? He's gone, left before lunch. Best really, no sentimental goodbyes and all that rubbish."

Fighting back a wave of nausea Lynn said: "What do you think he's going to do? Did you offer any cash to help him out?"

"No I didn't" said Richard, seeming to Lynn to be relishing his role as dragon slayer.

"What I did do however some weeks ago was to talk to George Minster, you remember him, one of my eldest and dearest friends and now editor in chief at the Telegraph. He and I had one of our liquid lunches and he mentioned the difficulty of finding inspirational journalistic talent. Look no further I said, your dream journalist is at hand."

"To cut to the quick, hot off the press so to speak, Gareth starts as a fully-fledged journalist with the Telegraph on Monday."

Lynn sat and stared at this man she married fifteen years ago and thought nothing will ever be the same again between us.

"You have done this for Gareth, in spite of..."

Mesmerised she looked at the slightly crumpled figure in front of her and thought you dear beautiful man, don't let me spoil this moment by even thinking of saying anything else.

Instead Lynn walked from her chair and sat on Richards lap. Her lips found his and she proceeded to give him the biggest tongue job he had had in his life.

She waited until she thought he'd recovered and placed his hand on her breast and started to undo the buttons on her blouse.

"Take me to bed now, love me like you've never loved me before and never let me out of your sight again."

Ten weeks later after fifteen years of trying, Lynn announced she was pregnant. Sophie was born after nine months of a born again marriage. Like all babies, their little girl was the most beautiful baby in the world.

Three years later she disappeared.

Chapter 2

It only took seconds to realise that their life's treasure was gone. As long as it took to load the supermarket groceries from the trolley into the boot of the car. A moment when their little girl was behind them and then was no more.

At first the Goodfellows perhaps naturally thought their little girl was having a bit of fun, hiding behind the other cars. But soon the cries of "Sophie, we're going" became "Sophie, stop playing games we're going." And then cries became shouts "Sophie come here this minute! Sophie!"

And then the heart stopping realisation she wasn't hiding under or behind the nearby cars. She wasn't hiding at all, she was gone. The two parents started running dementedly around the car park hoping she may have wandered off. A few shoppers paused to watch the couple but only when Lynn Goodfellow started to scream hysterically did they realise something was seriously, desperately wrong.

I don't think any journalist can ever describe the gut wrenching, sickening explosion of heart stopping emotion when a parent realises that it's their child that has disappeared. By now Lynn had been violently sick and was sobbing inconsolably, the sound was like the keening of an animal caught in a trap. Richard was still running madly around the car park, peering uselessly into cars making for the exit.

Finally a middle aged lady slowly approached Lynn and in heavily accented English, asked whether she could help.

"My girl. My baby, my everything has gone. Taken. I don't know. Oh God what can I do?"

It takes another mother only nanoseconds to take control.

"We must go to the supermarket office and call the police immediately."

After some initial confusion, after all, a small town Italian supermarket manager is not often confronted by sheer panic from a hysterical woman, Mario Chiesa finally understood the nature of the crisis and as a father himself, started shouting down the phone that the local police should come faster than they have ever moved before.

Francesco Andreotti, another father, who had often wondered how he would react if his child succumbed to the Italian penchant for raising money by kidnapping children, decided almost without thinking that his rank of Chief Inspector would move things along more decisively, arrived in a small convoy of police vehicles.

The nightmare of the next few days for the Goodfellows is beyond description. The Chief Inspector, already suspecting that their efforts to find the child alive are already beyond hope, tries to comfort them by drawing their attention to the spate of child kidnapping in Italy over the years, usually from wealthy families, and the safe return of the infant once the ransom is paid.

5 4

"In fact in the 1970's" he told them "In 1978 there were nearly 600 kidnappings. It was such a problem that the Italian government froze the assets of families where children had been abducted to discourage ransom demands."

Logic and reason do not really console and the inevitable intrusion of the world's press simply adds to the sense of isolation. Because he was a journalist himself, Richard Goodfellow found himself handling press conferences and TV interviews on his own, as Lynn retreated further and further into herself.

Although by now I was a senior journalist for the Telegraph, human interest stories were not my patch. My press awards had come from investigating scandals in the city and how the EC bureaucrats were prepared to pay any price to keep the common market roller coaster of civil service salaries, pensions, expenses, freebies, in fact, anything to squander tax payers money without being held accountable.

But I did send an email to George, the Managing Editor saying that as I had a personal knowledge of Richard and Lynn, perhaps I might be granted a face to face interview which they had refused to seemingly every other correspondent.

Richard and Lynn who were still seeking refuge in the holiday villa they had rented near Puglia (described in an iconic Italian kidnap film as famous for its 'beautiful ocean, nostalgic past, mafia, pizza and mandolins'), had made it clear in the few public appearances that they did not want to become cult Hello magazine style tragic characters.

George dropped by my desk and asked me to his office.

"Gareth you are one of our star reporters"

He was obviously struggling to find words to say and started fidgeting with his tie, his pencils, but finally it came out in a rush.

"Frankly your history with Richard and Lynn would make a personal interview with them at this time, which anyway I doubt they would grant, a less than sensitive intrusion. So the answer is no and do not go near this subject again."

I had sometimes wondered when George had been persuaded to offer me this job opportunity of a lifetime what had been said between these two oldest and dearest friends. Not only had Richard gone the extra mile for me, but clearly George had been dragged in too, but as a willing or unwilling accomplice, this I will never know. All I do know is that to repay the magnanimity of these two gentlemen is something I may never be given the opportunity to do. I left the office that night, got drunk, went home and for the first time in my life, cried proper tears to the selfish loss of not being able to help the Goodfellows in their misery.

Finally Richard and Lynn return home. He returned to work, Lynn devoted herself to charitable work and nothing is said of the day their world fell in on them.

After two years, with no ransom note and no body, the police draw a line under this case: 'Missing, presumed dead'.

Their neighbours gave them space, the press forgot about them and gradually they became non-people.

Chapter 3

Six years have passed by. I am now a very senior correspondent and as a reward (?) have been given the entire Middle East desk to run. You have to be joking! Have you ever been to Riyadh? But it houses one of the greatest centres of power in the Middle East, the Saudi royal family.

The city itself is a reflection of most Arab architecture, an eclectic mix of ultra-modern and ultra-traditional styles. There is no real poverty, but somehow the conservative style of dress still worn by most Saudis, still harkens back to life in the desert sands that surround the city, and their Bedouin ancestry. Although many social taboos have been either exiled or circumvented, the place of young girls and women generally is still imprisoned by the religious mores of the strict Wahhabi faith adhered to in the Saudi Kingdom.

Which is why I don't drink very much and haven't had a shag for years. But I do consume a lot of coffee! This morning I am sat in a new coffee shop located opposite a small modern building, the purpose of which is not clear. It's not quite midday so with the temperature already approaching 50°c (130°f) there are few people tempted to walk around. Since the presence of luxury sports cars, 4x4's, SUV's, opulent saloons and the like, is more common than Boris's Bikes, the arrival of three Porsche Cayennes outside the nearby building is hardly noteworthy.

Not until that is, eight or so chattering school girls emerge and start to cross the pavement. Judging by the 'heavies' accompanying them, these lasses seem to be special even by local standards. I cannot help staring, and then I stare again, and again, and again. If what I see is what I really see, I have almost solved the mystery of the universe!

After finishing my coffee, I take my cup inside and as casually as I can, ask the owner where the local Porsche dealer is, because having just seen the three opposite, this is now the car for me. Does ownership qualify me to go in the building opposite I ask jokily.

"Hardly" is the reply.

"That is a very private swimming pool reserved for ladies only of a very select group of Saudi families."

"Your coffee is excellent" I tell him, "I look forward to visiting you again, perhaps when the Porsches are here."

He grins and says "I wonder if it is the girls or cars you wish to gaze upon. Anyway they come every week, so ciao my perverted friend."

My mobile phone; is it a Blackberry, Blueberry, Apple Tart or Mince Pie? Don't ask me; all I know is that the camera has more pixels than pixiland. What's more I can sort of use it without looking obvious. So next week my girlie watching is recorded by Mr Samsung.

In the week that passed, my memory has gone into photographic overdrive. I know what I have seen and now I have the proof.

My Managing Editor is taken aback by my almost peremptory tone when I say to him "Do not even think of arguing or complaining about the cost, just send me the best undercover photographer you can lay your hands on. I will not say more on the phone, just do it."

I was not quite expecting a middle-aged slightly professorial man to appear at Riyadh airport. But what do I know how spook photographers look? We borrow a new Range Rover and the offside headlight is soon switched for a box of tricks which he had bought with him.

Now it's coffee time again and my new friend proudly brings me to the café door and parks his status symbol with a flourish. Like the café owner he is somewhat disturbed by my obvious interest in young nubile flesh, but George is paying him well enough to keep his prurient thoughts to himself.

Four hours later Albert and I are on a BA flight to London.

"George it is her, I know it now and I knew it from the moment my curiosity delved through my mental photographic archives."

"All I know is these girls are all members of one Saudi Royal family or another. At a guess they are all about 10 or 11 and the scenario fits. Girl abducted, girl sold, girl never seen again. Till now."

"Christ almighty, if you are right this will be the scoop of the century. But a photograph is not good enough. Sorry but we need a DNA match. If you succeed I will grant you possibly the greatest consolation prize you have ever been given. You can tell Richard and Lynn Goodfellow that their daughter Sophie is alive and well."

Mr Google's internet tells me all I need to know about DNA. He doesn't actually say how to obtain relevant test samples from a Saudi princess. Can I persuade her to suck a lollipop or nose bleed over my jacket? In the end it simply boils down to cash. One of the pool cleaners is a typical Filipino employee in Saudi: badly paid, cruelly treated; is persuaded by more money than she has earned in the past five years to steal hairs from a comb in the sports bag laying in the changing room. A bag with the name Farah al Sidi bin Saud clearly printed on it.

We wait for the results from the Metropolitan Police laboratory, where all Sophie's records shared with the Italian police were kept, with an impatience bordering on hysteria. But I knew I could never be mistaken so I sort of felt a sense of déjà vu when my certainty was confirmed. The greatest news story in decades lay within our grasp. The real catch is what to do with it. Clearly an explosive story now will simply result in Farah aka Sophie never being seen again. The best story will be when after she is reunited with her parents and the full dramatic tale can be exposed.

Chapter 4

The British Embassy in the Kingdom of Saudi Arabia occupies a gated compound which houses all the diplomatic offices required to service such a 'prestigious' posting. Perhaps the biggest department belongs to the commercial press and information Station Chief. Martin Hancock, if that is even his real name, controls a ne'er do collection of press officers who strangely enough look more like SAS troopers than West End PR luvvies. Probably because that's what they are. Ever since the link between Osama Bin Laden, Al Qaeda and the Saudis became public, Saudi Arabia has become front line in the offensive by the Brits and the USA to monitor and track down any threat to the West from Islamic terrorists in the Middle East.

My task is to persuade the Ambassador and his Press Chief to come up with a plan to rescue our fair maiden and return her to the bosom of her true family. But how on earth have we arrived at this crazy situation? Simply because Al Qaeda in Britain themselves monitor the daily goings and comings of anyone they regard significant enough to do harm to their cause. Journalists are high on this list as they shift public opinion like changes in the weather. Right wing papers like the Telegraph carry significant punch with middle class opinion. These 'not in my back garden' do-gooders some might say, unfortunately are the backbone of the UK teaching, legal, political and business management professions. They read the Telegraph and consequently view with deep mistrust anything that isn't 'British', especially the Arabs.

So they watch and wait hoping for anything which might discredit these newspaper gurus. By association, Richard Goodfellow's regular lunches with George Minster made him a target. The holiday in Italy came as a sort of bonus. But what to do with it. Their Red Brigade partners, nowadays underground in Italy, had no doubts. Strike a blow against these hated imperialists, steal a child: ransom it, kill it, sell it, anything.

By strange coincidence news of the abduction reached Sheik Sidi bin Saud as his wife of 10 years was bitterly complaining that he was infertile as a eunuch. This child would be theirs! His close contacts with Al Qaeda soon enabled the little girl to be smuggled from Italy. As does happen, the arrival of one child broke the barren chains and over the next few years the Sheik and his wife had a real brother and sister for their 'adopted' princess.

You may hate their politics, their calculated cruelty to anyone who stands in their way, but even the most vicious cold blooded murdering villain is the father of quite often, a very happy family. Quite literally the Sheik would go to any lengths to protect his wife and children.

Thus our meeting started with the basic premise that to approach the family and ask for our 'toy' back was a non-starter. She would disappear, so too probably would our newspaper office, likely too the embassy staff would be declared persona non grata and deported.

So tit for tat, sauce for the goose and all that bollocks! A cunning plan was all that was needed, along with a few volunteers and hey presto the girl was ours.

My brief was simple: sit and have coffee and phone our lads the moment the girls hit the pavement. At that moment a huge bang erupted inside a Range Rover parked opposite. An Arab then came flying round the corner screaming and shouting that a terrorist attack was starting and everyone to scatter. A second bang convinced everyone that panic was entirely in order, the girls and their guards totally unsure what to do started running away from their cars. At which point a nondescript van with an open side door charged along the street and four arms reached out and bingo, the job was done. The van went no distance into an alley which backed onto nothing. Within seconds the girl now bound and taped was bundled into the back of an executive car with diplomatic number plates. Minutes later it swept into the Embassy compound.

The British Ambassador, who saw his future hanging by a thread, wanted the girl gone before the Saudi's realised what had happened. But it was already too late. Within minutes of the capture Riyadh was in lockdown. Every car, lorry and bus was held at gunpoint and searched. Roads exiting the city were sealed and the railway station and international airport closed to exiting flights and trains.

Perhaps it's no great surprise that the Embassy too had its own undercover Saudi infiltrator. Barely fifteen minutes passed before information reached the Saudi secret service that the girl at the centre of the furore was within the Embassy walls.

What a cataclysmic mess! The Ambassador was called immediately to the palace and told in no uncertain terms that the girl should be surrendered or the consequences would be so severe as to be unimaginable.

So with the cat well and truly out of the bag, there was absolutely no reason why the Telegraph should not publish the story of the century. So my story hit the pages next day. Stuck inside the compound, there was no opportunity to tell the Goodfellows in person, but George, my editor was as good as his word and let me phone them beforehand with the news that I had found their daughter alive and well. This was before the Embassy phones were cut off after the story broke.

International sentiment rallied to the cause and the Saudis soon were under no illusion that a rescue attempt by invading the diplomatic immunity of the compound would be totally unacceptable.

Jesus! What a standoff!

The Saudi Ambassador in London was given an audience with the Prime Minister.

"If this is allowed to continue, we reserve the right to cancel every economic and military tie with United Kingdom. We will seize the assets of every British company operating in the country and suspend all contracts with UK suppliers. This will include the order for 50 fighter jets for the Saudi Air force."

Chapter 5

"The loss would run into thousands of millions, if not billions of pounds." The PM told a hastily convened cabinet meeting.

"All for the sake of one child", said one cabinet member.

"Surely the Goodfellows can be made to realise that the loss of their daughter, who after all, is alive and well, must be seen in the national interest, above petty parental concerns."

This started a heated row rarely seen in cabinet meetings. Insults were traded with barely concealed venom as ministers became bitterly divided over how to respond to the Saudi ultimatum. In the end the PM called a halt and said he would reflect on everything that had been said and reach a decision himself the following day.

That night over dinner in the No.10 flat James Guthrie recounted the row to his wife.

"As a parent, frankly, I am torn completely by this looming abyss. Sort of doomed if I do and doomed if I don't."

"Darling, you must do what you think best for the Goodfellows and the country, but I agree, I don't think they are compatible. Let me ask you as the father of our own beautiful daughter. When she was diagnosed with leukaemia, if the choice had been her life instead of your political career, which would you have chosen?"

At a press conference the following morning a very haggard and clearly emotionally exhausted Prime Minister made the following statement:

"After considering all the implications of this tragic situation, I have determined that to surrender a girl's life with her real parents by conceding to economic blackmail cannot be morally, ethical or diplomatically acceptable. Sophie Goodfellow must be bought home and reunited with her true parents. The Saudi's must square their conscience as best they can with the economic and political consequences of their threats. They are the ones whose original outrageous behaviour triggered this affair. To sacrifice the livelihoods of thousands of totally innocent UK citizens simply underlines the complete lack of moral standards displayed by the Saudi Royal Family."

Well, that's told them in no uncertain terms, hasn't it?! If diplomacy is the art of telling someone an unpalatable truth without upsetting them, this is definitely not a star example.

So a flood of cancelled orders, BP nationalised, British assets seized, bank accounts closed, in a word, economic meltdown ensues.

However, internationally the Saudi's are under pressure to release the girl. Diplomatic condemnation from the United Nations and other subtle forms of persuasion finally results in them bowing to the inevitable and announcing that the child can be flown back to the UK.

But even this is not without further humiliation for the UK government. The Saudi's insist that she will only be allowed to travel to the airport in the Ambassador's diplomatic CD car along with the Ambassador and press representative. A specially chartered BA flight will be given permission to land and the entourage will board the plane well away from the terminal building where the public and press corps would have a field day. Furthermore, the Ambassador will fly to the UK and not return as the Embassy will be closed once the flight has departed.

I am observing all this at first hand as I too cannot leave the compound except with the Ambassador. Perhaps the most unsettling aspect of our isolation is the behaviour of Farah nee Sophie herself. She is all at once reserved, aloof, withdrawn, detached, speaking only when spoken to and then in her clear, slightly accented English only answering with the absolute minimal replies. After all, no one gave her any choice in the matter. Perhaps she too feels hijacked as a pawn in some unfathomable adult game.

It is a clear and sunny day (are there any other in Saudi?) as our cavalcade moves out of the Embassy Compound and flanked by Saudi military and police outriders travels at high speed along cleared streets to the airport. There parked as far away as possible is a BA 777 with boarding steps surrounded by even more heavily armed soldiers. I have a feeling that we are not going to be given a farewell box of chocolates.

Without any welcoming gestures we are ushered to our seats by a grim looking cabin crew. This flight is not their choice and one can see them hoping that the Saudi's have not doctored the top up petrol with sugar!

It is not until we are seated and belted up that the Captain tells us that our expected take off time is in one hour. So we can move around the plane. I take the chance to go and sit next to Farah, who stares at me with eyes that make me feel I've crawled from under a stone.

Without waiting to say hello she says "Are you the man who has taken me away from my family?"

I am so taken aback at this accusation from this ice-cold ten year old that I find it difficult to compose a reply. In the end I say that I am a newspaper reporter and find things out and report them. What other people do about my stories is not under my control.

I squirm as she says "Well, now you have spoken to me, you can report that."

This from a girl 10 going on 30.

I am rejected, not wanted, am undesirable in her world.

So I return to my seat near the Ambassador and ask him how he thinks things are going. His voice is cold and remote as he says "Gareth, you must understand that your extraordinary skill in uncovering this story has led to consequences which are spiralling out of control. You may be journalist of the year, win a Pulitzer or whatever, but for the rest of us left to pick up the fallout, you are decidedly not the flavour of the month."

And so it falls into place. Ever since my story broke I have detected a coolness from my friends, colleagues and even my editor who has never experienced circulation figures like it in his life. I am a sort of pariah. Who said 'a prophet is never loved in his own land?'

Pointless trying to continue this conversation, I belt back up and wait.

At precisely 2pm our BA flight is given clearance from the control tower to take off. There is an almost palpable sigh of relief that there are to be no last minute security or customs glitches. Our diplomatic immunity has won through, and our prize is on her way home. There is a flight time of 1 hour 20 minutes to leave Saudi airspace.

At precisely 11am in London the Saudi Ambassador is ushered into the Prime Minister's office in 10 Downing Street.

"I have to inform you sir, that I am instructed by the Lord Anointed King of Saudi Arabia that due to the totally illegal kidnapping of a Saudi citizen the Kingdom of Saudi Arabia is now at war with the United Kingdom. Your citizens have 24 hours with which to leave the Kingdom or risk internment until hostilities cease."

It took the PM nearly a minute to register the reality of what had just been said. To say that his mouth literally dropped open would be putting it mildly.

James Guthrie's initial reaction was simply to say "You <u>have</u> to be joking."

But realising that the Ambassador was in deadly earnest, realised something more diplomatic was required.

"There is nothing illegal, Ambassador, about returning a natural born British citizen to the home of her birth. I cannot believe that this action can change the legality of that."

"On the contrary Prime Minister, Princess Farah is the legitimately adopted daughter of a Saudi family and as such a citizen of the Kingdom."

"But the photographs and DNA tests prove that Sophie is who we say she is."

"I am afraid Prime Minister we accept neither as proof. Photographs can easily be electronically altered and it is a proven fact that DNA testing has led to many innocent people being convicted and vice versa."

"This is preposterous", exclaimed the PM finally exasperated by the bland self-satisfied smug look on the Ambassador's face. "I will phone the King immediately and demand an explanation of this totally prefabricated justification for a declaration of war."

"There is a comedy film called 'The Mouse that Roared' with Peter Sellers", the Prime Minister by now had thrown diplomatic nicety to the wind; "I suggest you go and watch it. In the meantime I must ask you to leave so I can contact your head of state."

"Unfortunately, Prime Minister, I have to tell you before I give my respectful farewell, that the King is today in what you would call prayerful retreat and cannot be contacted. Goodbye, the affairs of the Saudi Embassy will be handled by the Swiss legation until this sad state of affairs is resolved."

Chapter 6

BA Captain Tim Murdoch settled into the flight routine with his 1st officer co-pilot James Saunders. They had a routing agreed with Saudi air control to fly North West to the Saudi coast before heading to the Gulf of Aqaba, passing over the Suez Canal before entering the Mediterranean Sea with a further 3 hour flight to London.

The cabin crew started moving down the plane taking orders for drinks before serving a late lunch. There was now little conversation and with so few people aboard a plane capable of carrying over 300 people there was an air of being the last remaining people alive on the planet.

Ten minutes into the flight the Captain realised that they weren't. The shockwaves from two military jets caused the 777 to shudder and as they settled into formation either side of the cockpit, the port side military pilot was able to indicate with his hands that the Captain should communicate by radio.

"Good afternoon Captain, I am Lieutenant Faisal of the Saudi Air Force. I have to inform you that as of 10 minutes ago the Kingdom of Saudi Arabia is at war with the United Kingdom. You are therefore a hostile plane flying through Saudi airspace. My instructions are to allow you five minutes to confirm by satellite phone that this is correct, and then for you to follow me to my military airbase where you will be held in confinement until hostilities cease. Failure to comply will result in the destruction of your aircraft. Do not even think that this is how you say in English, 'a bluff'. My orders are clear and you are an enemy plane flying over Saudi national territory."

Even whilst this exchange was going on, James Saunders the young co-pilot had already patched through the satellite link to London.

"Incredible as it seems", he told the Captain "it's true."

"Ok James", said Tim "I am the Captain of this flight and will make the final decision, but first I would respect your opinion."

After a moment's thought James said "I think it's fairly clear the Saudi's have concocted this plan with the simple intention that if they do not have Princess Farah back, no one else will. My take is that the Saudi's intend to carry out this threat and if we don't comply, we are dead."

"Let the cockpit voice recorder state that I, Captain Murdoch, had already made the decision to accede to the Saudi order. My co-pilot has reaffirmed the threat that we will not leave Saudi airspace alive. We are therefore diverting to our new destination."

With a waggle of his wings the Saudi pilot turned to the new course and a fresh Saudi ground controller issued new bearings and GPS landing reference.

"I am sorry to tell you" announced the Captain over the PA system "that we are obliged to return to a military airbase as a state of war now exists between our two countries. The option of being shot down as a hostile intruder is not an option."

So without a shot being fired, or diplomatic immunity compromised, Princess Farah is on her way 'back home' for a second time. Nothing is said in the plane until finally the Ambassador says what everyone else is thinking.

"Well my boy, I hope by now your journalist's appetite for sensation is truly satisfied. Perhaps we should get the alcohol off the tray tables in front of us before we give the Saudi's even more reason to imprison us."

After talking the Boeing 777 down, the Captain is instructed to proceed to the furthest end of the military runway.

"Captain, please open the forward door over the steps, once in place, and allow Princess Farah to exit the plane alone only accompanied by one stewardess for her safety to the bottom of the stairs. She will be followed by the journalist Gareth Richards. The remaining passengers and crew will await a convoy to escort them to where they will be held under house arrest until further arrangements can be made."

It is a prearranged journalistic bun fight. The moment Princess Farah is free of the stewardess's steadying arm two little figures detach themselves from the rank of photographers lined up some 50 yards away. They hurtle across the runway and throw themselves into Farah's open arms. The huge smiles, the tears are genuine. "Where have you been we have been so worried? We've missed you. Mummy and Daddy are in a real tiz." The little Arabic voices reach the cameras and sound equipment strategically placed to record every word and drama of this reunion. Finally the parents join in this love fest before the family is taken away in, ironically, a Bentley limo.

And I know why I am here. I am the only British journalist present. I am the only one who can record for the UK public the family joy at being together again. Me, the one that started all this, thinking that this will be one of the most dramatic kidnap rescues of all time, is being forced to witness how much humble pie I must eat. Telegraph circulation figures will once again go through the roof. But I may never trust my instincts again.

However, I am a reporter first and last and so the story is told as factually and unemotionally as I can. If the headline 'Love wins through' sticks in my throat, the world's media swallow it hook, line and sinker.

In the immediate aftermath of the welcoming Saudi press circus, I am taken away to a secure address in the centre of Riyadh. Only days later I can break the news, the world is relieved to hear that World War III between the Kingdom and Great Britain is now over and diplomatic relations can be repaired and healed.

A lengthy correspondence by phone and email with my editor suggests that my days as Middle East correspondent for the Telegraph are numbered. I am not inclined to argue that my personal credibility has been damaged beyond repair. Time to pack my bags, and hopefully be given a new assignment, preferably as far away as possible from sand and young girls.

It is therefore with some consternation that I am summoned to an audience with Farah's father. He tells me that he and his wife wish to lay this trauma to rest once and for all. Since I am supposedly this long term friend could I invite Richard and Lynn Goodfellow to the Kingdom to finally judge for themselves the hurt and confusion this has caused his family. It is now up to Farah to decide which is her real family.

I know before I start that this is the opening of yet another heartbreak hotel, yet how can I refuse them a final chance to even just see their precious daughter. So they come and in the unsurpassed splendour of the palace Farah surrounded by clinging hands of her sibling brother and sister, meet her parents.

They are at once awed and crushed by their surroundings. Chestnut Avenue, Haselmere in Surrey, ill prepares you for the sheer scale of opulence which confronts you every direction you look.

Once again I am asked to witness the meeting as a 'friend' of the family. Once again, Farah's cool clear diction reduces all emotion to dust.

"Thank you for coming, you have now seen my home and family for yourselves. You are people I do not know from a strange land, whose people tried to take me away. Perhaps you can now finally leave us in peace."

Richard, Lynn and I are given the 5 cent tour of the parts of the palace we haven't already seen, including Farah's own suite, and depart numbed. Lynn managed one tearful farewell as she whispered "you are still our daughter and we will always love you."

I can hardly remember the journey back to the airport as Lynn and Richard sit silent yet bonded in a physical and emotional embrace that I cannot intrude upon.

Their daughter is gone for a second time.

So the years again pass. I am forgiven and return to the city beat. Richard and Lynn live their lives as normally as busy people do. Only the framed photo of their 3 year old daughter sitting on the mantelpiece is evidence of the vacuum in their existence that never gets filled. Each year on her birthday they do rekindle their shared emptiness, knowing that it reopens all the hurt they should be best putting behind them. They send her a birthday card just signed with their names, never knowing whether since they never come back marked 'return to sender' is a sign that they reach her or are intercepted and destroyed.

It is now eight years later and I have become comfortably friendly with Richard and Lynn. We never talk about my part in the past. We are beyond blame and recriminations. I now have a longstanding girlfriend but whether it has been my brush with this family tragedy I cannot tell, but I have never wished to have children of my own. We share holidays and weekends together, but my gaze is always drawn to that photo on the mantelpiece.

Life in the Kingdom also moves on. Women, as in many Arab countries are gaining more responsibility, demanding and getting access to better and higher education. Farah is no exception. Shopping trips to the West End, a richly rewarding feature for Harrods, unloading the unlimited credit cards held by these Arabian shopaholics, has been superseded by a place at Oxford University.

Tall, slim, dark brown hair, deep brown eyes (inherited from her mother) and softly tanned skin, Farah is drop dead gorgeous. She shares a comfortable flat in the city with an ex Cheltenham Ladies College girl, known as 'Fritz'. It is not long before Farah and Fritz are a regular part of the social scene. Farah's bodyguard does his best to keep in tow but following her new Mini Cooper S is not always easy. Farah for the first time in her life is liberated from the strict religious and social conventions which governed her life at home.

But the two of them are genuinely nice, generous cheerleaders. So into this second term Fritz is upset when Farah seems to withdraw from their friendship. However she is not one to let a chum down and when Farah asks if she can borrow her beaten up Peugeot 207 for the day she shrugs her shoulders and throws her the keys.

"I am sorry, sweet" says Farah "I have been a real cow lately but I will make it up. It's just that I have to see some people and I would prefer to travel without Oddjob following me."

Fritz grinned and said "Well promise me that I'll be let in on the secret one day."

"One day" says Farah, "I will."

A middle aged couple, working in the front garden weeding, trimming, watering, planting as one does on a lazy Saturday afternoon, are curious when a battered Peugeot 207 pulls up outside the front gates to their drive. Their curiosity is more bemused and attentive when an attractive teenager in polo shirt and jeans tentatively pushes the gate open and walks up the drive.

"Hello", says the girl hesitantly.

"I don't suppose you remember me. I am Sophie."

Richard and Lynn Goodfellow move together as if an apparition has materialised. The girl looks at this couple who are now holding hands, because saying something seems beyond them.

"I don't know whether you can help me" she begins "I know it's not fair to ask", she plunges on fearful if she stops she will turn and flee.

"I am in trouble and I don't know anyone else who I can turn to."

Her voice trails miserably off.

"I am pregnant."

Lynn Goodfellow whispers "Oh my dear child".

She opens her arms and folds Sophie into her breast. Nothing has ever prepared Richard for anything like this in his life. So he too gathers both of them up with tears streaming down his face. There are tears and cuddles, hugs kisses and tears, tears and cuddles, hugs and kisses and more tears.

Their daughter has finally come home.

The End

THE RUNAWAY SUB

Prologue

Four young men towing a good sized rib behind a camper van is not an unusual sight in Dover docks. But the contents of one of the suitcases may have raised a few eyebrows if opened.

The journey down through France to the south coast was uneventful. So too, was launching the boat from a secluded beach and anchoring it overnight.

The following morning three of the four donned wet suits and diving gear and enjoyed the trip round the headland into the adjoining bay.

The return journey to England was equally without drama and a good price was obtained for the rib. The campervan was returned to the rental company who although slightly surprised, gave no real thought to the higher than average mileage.

Between Nice and Monaco on the Mediterranean coast of France lays the pretty resort of Villefranche. It retains much of the architecture and character of centuries gone by. The narrow streets run higgledy-piggledy up and down, joined by paths and shaded mature trees.

Down by the small fishing harbour is the chapel of St Peter, a fisherman's chapel that was given to Jean Cocteau in 1957 to decorate. His simple outlined figures, traced in geometrical fashion make a refreshing change from the density of frescoes that usually greet one in Catholic churches.

Along the waterfront are a myriad number of restaurants side by side with wonderful views to Cap Ferrat over the water.

Next to the harbour is the Citadel that was built by the Duke of Savoy to guard the port from unwelcome visitors, pirates!

Today the views from the ramparts welcome visitors who bring much more welcome trade and business to the shops, bars and restaurants in the port.

These visitors unlike those from the past do not row ashore from Roman triremes, Arab Dhows or Phoenician galleys, but in motorised lifeboats from the dozens of cruise ships which anchor in the bay every season. Sometimes up to four ships disgorge literally thousands of passengers from all over the world, but not today. Only two ships lay peacefully at anchor, basking in a perfect Mediterranean sun.

The MV Fairy Princess is a 76,000 ton Panamanian registered ship built some five years ago and is home to some 2500 passengers and 1200 crew. Nearby the older and smaller Holiday Magic, only 49000 tons, is a baby compared to the leviathans that ply the fast growing holiday cruise trade, with new ships over 150,000 tons carrying in excess of 5,000 passengers and 2000 crew.

The two captains have been friends for thirty years and almost unusually are both British. But they know this is about to change as both are rapidly reaching retirement age and then replacements are just as likely to be Italian, Greek or Scandinavian. No one seems to trust the Asians or Orientals to skipper their boats, although increasingly the crew and passengers are from these parts.

All of these thoughts are voiced by the two ageing seafarers, for whom returning to their wives on a more permanent footing is perhaps more daunting than retirement itself. Edward Dauntless, captain of the Fairy Princess and today's lunchtime host, reaches over to light his companion's cigar.

"One small privilege of being skipper is they can't stop you smoking in your own dining room".

"Don't worry", replies Captain James Samson, "It's only a matter of time, but hopefully we won't be around to see it".

Their conversation resumes over vintage port and brandy amidst a cloud of cigar smoke. Hobbies never pursued, holidays never taken, families often distant memories, all this is about to change, so four dull thuds barely intrude on their preoccupation with the future.

They are both slightly affronted when the doors of the dining saloon burst open and Pep the captain's steward rushes in and in his excitement forgets all his usual deference and shouts: "Captain, Captain, your ship, she is sinking".

"Nonsense" says Samson, "have you been drinking?"

"Is true, is true, come look!"

The two captains, reluctant to be panicked, but nevertheless are intrigued by Pep's insistence; start to rise when Samson's mobile phone rings.

"Sir, it's first officer Greenway here, I think you should return to the ship as she is sinking and I have given the order to abandon ship. We have probably thirty minutes before we settle on the bottom."

They both rush outside to the bridge deck and an amazing sight meets their eyes. A small armada of orange lifeboats is clustered around the sides of Holiday Magic and the crew and few remaining passengers, all kitted up in their orange lifejackets, are clambering on board.

"Thanks for lunch Edward, probably the most memorable one I've ever had. Looks like my retirement is closer to the horizon than we thought!"

"Best of luck Jim, God knows how this can have happened. Your First seems to have everything under control but let me know immediately if there is any further assistance I can give."

Looking every inch the senior captain in his dress uniform, tanned face with mutton chops and moustache, Captain Samson motors back in his own lifeboat, painfully aware that disaster has happened on his watch and nothing can be done to save his doomed ship.

But of course, anchored in only 20 metres of water, Holiday Magic is not going to disappear into a watery grave. The Captain and First Officer are still on the bridge as the superstructure remains clearly visible above the waterline.

"I'm guessing four simultaneous detonations under the keel, with no chance the pumps could cope with the flood of water coming in. In any case, once the level of water in the engine room blew all the electrics nothing worked anymore.

Regardless, fortunately, with only a skeleton crew of engineers on duty, they were all able to escape without harm" said Greenway.

"So we've lost no one and no reported injuries. Thank God for small mercies." James Samson surveyed the decks of his ship and wondered, as did all his crew and passengers, what on earth sabotaging a cruise liner could possibly achieve.

Sitting in their luxuriously panelled boardroom, none of the Directors of the Pegasus Cruise Lines had any better idea either. Ben Attwood the CEO waved his perfectly manicured hands around as if to pick the answer out of the air.

"At least the insurers aren't shitting us, and have agreed to pay for refloating and refurbing, but only because they can't use the no-terrorist clause to indemnify themselves. And we sure as hell can't shift the blame to the Captain or crew. So, who is to blame?"

"What about a disgruntled ex-employee?" asked Curtis Greenhaugh, a non-executive director, whose job it was to supervise the on-board theatre entertainment.

"What, one of your fired ballet dancers, caught diddling a passenger's son? Be real Curtis, this is the job of a professional saboteur, not some tutued fairy."

"Only a thought," sulked Greenhaugh.

"What about a competitor trying to put us out of business? Competition out there is very fierce; this could be a case of cut-throat piracy on the high seas."

This suggestion from Tom Lamplugh, the Finance Director, was met with a mixed reaction of incredulity and scorn.

After an hour of pointless arguing, Ben Attwood finally called a halt and told them that the insurer's own fraud investigation team was fully committed to solving the problem. Until they could unravel the mystery, anything else was pure speculation.

Two days later a letter was delivered to the Pegasus Cruise Line in their Liverpool Street offices.

"Remember the MV Holiday Magic" it simply read. "We have the resources, we have the technology, next time we want the money. Don't even think we cannot make it happen. TCC."

"Four limpet mines, strategically placed along the hull sank the ship. Who and where from is anyone's guess but our opinion is that you don't mess with these guys if they threaten again."

The Marine Surveyor left Ben Attwood's office just before their insurers rang to say they had received a copy of the report and were considering amendments to the company's policy in case there was a serial ship wrecker targeting Pegasus Cruises.

It wasn't long before all the cruise liner owners were confronted with similar warnings from their insurers.

Chapter 1

Devon is one of the most beautiful counties in Great Britain. It has many of the most picturesque harbours and villages ever painted. And it has a nuclear submarine base in Devonport. Perhaps a tad less romantic but nevertheless as much a part of Britain's security as the seas around the coast.

Burntwood Cottage lies down a lane near to Peter Tavy, a typical village on the edge of Dartmoor, a few miles from Tavistock and twenty miles from Plymouth and Devonport.

Commander Richard Nelson reflected on his life, as he often did driving into work, that it couldn't be much better: skipper of a nuclear attack submarine at the age of thirty-five, a beautiful home and a stunning and equally talented wife – a paediatrician at the local Derriford hospital. The world according to the gospel of Richard Nelson was PDG. He had met Claire while still at Dartmouth Naval College and they had been together ever since. The only rival for her affections had been his roommate, and now first mate, Colin McAndrew. Having beaten off the competition it wasn't long before they married. Despite the fact they had been unable to have children, Richard's love for his wife was like his namesake's column in Trafalgar Square: tall, singular and there forever. Well, then there was the Navy of course. A different love, but a devotion inspired by a real sense of patriotism together with the huge bonus that it was surrounded by huge dollops of seawater.

But this morning was different. Instead of the daily commute to Devonport, whilst his sub was undergoing some repairs, Richard had been summoned to the MOD in London. People often think that nuclear ships and submarines are new technology. This is not really true. HM Submarine Torch had been first put on the Naval architects drawing board in 1965, and actually launched four years later in 1969. Many of the dials are still analogue not digital and stuffing comes out of the hydroplane operators chair. So repairs and 'make do', in these straightened economic times, are a regular part of these ageing submarine's lives.

"Why don't you drive to London darling, it will do you and the car good to go for a spin. I don't mind if you spend the night at the Navy Club and have a bit of fun with your old buddies."

"Well, if you're sure. I'll leave early tomorrow and come back on Wednesday."

So this morning is different.

"Love you, be good." Richard waves as he navigates around potholes in their lane. Claire smiles and says "I'll be very good, don't you worry."

Chapter 2

Rear Admiral Howard Cruikshank is dashing, debonair and a right royal pain in the ass to many who have dealings with him. But none can deny his meteoric rise to his rank at the age of fifty. Fast tracked from Naval College to an engineering masters degree in University, his experience with nuclear propulsion created for him an almost unique niche role in the 21st century Royal Navy. His transfer from engineering rank to bridge command was equally unprecedented, so few people were surprised when he joined to brass hats at the MOD in London.

Unfortunately, with seniority often comes superiority, and alone amongst the other top bananas he often wore full dress uniform to work, particularly when interviewing lower ranks. Such as this morning.

After keeping Commander Nelson waiting for a demoralising thirty minutes he was ushered into the Admiral's chamber. Feeling dowdy in his drab Marks and Spencers civvy suit, his spirits were not improved as the Admiral said "Shan't keep you long Nelson, busy schedule and all that".

"Yes Sir, I appreciate your time".

"Well, do you now, you may be not so appreciative of my news. The reality of today's Navy is that it is caught between the upper and nether millstone of dramatic improvements in weapons technology and the means of delivery, balanced by the sheer cost of these improvements and the budget cuts imposed by the government. Our new nuclear submarines cost £2 billion each as are two new aircraft carriers. So where does that leave us? Cut out the redundant blunt cutlasses and rely on super slim rapier swords. So, to put it in a nutshell, our oldest fleet of nuclear submarines has to be decommissioned and unfortunately, Commander, that includes yours. After your last routine patrol, once existing repairs are completed, your submarine and crew will be stood down. I felt that I and the Navy owed you at least this much to tell you personally, and how we regret the necessity for this action."

"Do you mean that we are all redundant, I mean literally we will be jobless, out of work, washed up on the beach, just like that?"

Richard could barely choke the words out. In the overheated office his shirt began sticking to his back as perspiration leaked out of every pore.

"What about our careers, the sacrifices of many of the lower ranks to stay in the Navy? Don't we count for anything?"

The Admiral shifted uncomfortably. "I'm afraid the decision is out of my hands".

Richard stood and replied: "No it's not, you've not given us a chance to prove ourselves. What about the new submarines that are being built, don't we qualify for those?"

"I'm afraid not Commander, new officers and crews have already been selected and it is not for you query the merits or demerits of the navy's choice."

"You mean your choice!"

Richard was on his feet shouting.

"We never had a chance. You probably trashed our chances from day one. I bet the new commander is a relative or a friend of a friend".

His voice trailed off as the Admiral's office door burst open and two security guards, alerted by the ruckus, rushed in and queried if everything was ok.

The Admiral stood behind his desk and said they could go. There was no need to panic as the Commander was about to leave.

He stared at Richard and said coldly, "Commander you will leave now. I will pretend that I did not hear that preposterous outburst. But I do understand that you are emotionally overwrought. Do not try my patience further or you will not be returning to your last command but will be locked in the brig. And you will salute before you exit my office."

After raising his hand in salute, Richard barely perceptibly said: "Aye Aye Sir, But I still cannot believe what you've done to ninety-eight of Her Majesty's finest Naval Officers and crew".

"Go", thundered the Admiral, "before God I have you arrested for insubordination."

The outer office was silent as Commander Nelson walked through. The security guards hovered uncertainly as if expecting a final rear guard action. But with a final nod, Richard walked out, unsighted, to the embarrassed glances of the office staff who knew that their bastard of a boss had just reduced another fellow being to ashes.

Blindly walking down Whitehall, Richard blundered into passers-by, tourists, office girls, men in smart suits, London's great unwashed, black or white it didn't register. Some stepped aside, some pushed back, some said "hey man, watch where you're going." Others: "Are you pissed or stoned?" A few, but very few, saw a man crushed by the misery of defeat and wondered for a moment before the world reclaimed them, what inner turmoil was reflected in such a face of abject failure.

A walk in Green Park did nothing to soothe the soul. More anger, more rage coagulated into a solid lead block of frustration and almost incoherent impotence.

His car, when he finally reached it, seemed to mock him as if to say, "You were never good enough for me, and now you've proved it".

No naval club tonight. Richard knew he could not face his fellow sailors even if they did not yet know of the doomsday end to his career.

Driving like an automaton, Richard found the M4 and ultimately joined the M5. Plan A was dead, Plan B had never even been considered. Approaching Exeter Richard finally brought himself up short and realised he was in no state to return home and face his wife.

The sign for the turnoff on the A38 to Buckfastleigh suddenly awakened memories of his early days of courtship where evening of drinks, dinner and sometimes overnight passion, meant at least a glass to drown his sorrows in a familiar tavern where at least his shame would not yet be public.

SHAME. The word burned in his brain. It wasn't even his fault but every fibre of his being told him that every finger pointed at him, from now on he would be his military decoration of failure.

Two hours later, the Landlord realised the young, well-spoken, quiet gentleman who had steadily consumed the best part of a half bottle of scotch was hunting for his car keys on the bar.

"I am sorry Sir, I have no idea what kind of dragons you are fighting, but you are not driving away from this bar. There is a room available and you will take it, otherwise I shall call the police and their overnight accommodation is a lot less comfortable and the consequences far more expensive."

"I am so sorry", Richard stumbled behind the manager and clutched the bannister rail. He refused the offer of food and as the bedroom door opened, wiped tears from his eyes.

"It's not been a good day, but thanks for being my good Samaritan".

The manager held his arm and said quietly:

"I've been there myself; you just have to rediscover who you really are. Goodnight Sir, I am sure things will seem a bit better in the morning."

Chapter 3

The Abbey Inn has the typical charm of a real Devon bar restaurant and hotel. It's quaint, it's old, it's picturesque and several of the rooms peer out over the car park beside the River Dart.

Knowing that he was in no mood to sleep and that more alcohol was not the answer (what was the question?), Richard wandered across the bedroom. The smells of a typical Devon countryside evening greeted him as he opened the window overlooking the car park. Still only quarter to ten, vehicles were still coming and going.

The throaty exhaust note of a Porsche Carerra vaguely registered in his memory as a car belonging to someone he sort of knew.

It parked under a lamp and recognition dawned as the tall, square frame of his mornings Admiral extricated itself from the driver's seat. The girl who emerged from the passenger side was also reminiscent of someone he also knew.

She linked her arm through the Admiral's and looked up to give him a hugging kiss. Her throaty laugh sighed up to the bedroom window. Richard realised with certainty why he knew the girl…it was his wife.

They walked arm in arm into the hotel and ten minutes later Richard heard them chuckling as they passed his bedroom door. The room swam in shards of light as the final pillars of his life crashed around him. He realised he had no will, no energy, no rage enough to charge into a confrontation. If agony is a bottomless pit, Richard was still falling when he vomited the scotch into the toilet pan.

Curled up on the bed in the foetal position of a baby not wanting to face the real world, Richard finally slept. With his tears still soaking the pillowcase, he came too just after 6am. Old disciplines die hard, so after a shower he reached the hotel desk just after 6.30.

The young night porter took his credit card without comment about his early departure. One look at the unshaven, haggard face in front of him told him that missing breakfast was the least of this guest's problems.

Richard finally coughed and said: "I'm sorry but I haven't been well and I may be mistaken but last night two guests arrived late and they may be acquaintances of mine. I would like to leave a note under their windscreen wiper."

"Oh lovely couple", replied the porter, "been coming here now regularly for over a year, longer maybe, but I've only been here fifteen months myself. Super car.... are you ok Sir?", the porter asked anxiously as Richard's body seemed to convulse as if he was having a heart attack.

"No. no, I'm fine, just a bit too much to drink last night".

"Well, I'm off duty at 7 so I won't see your friends, but say hello to them from me when you next see them", said the porter.

Fortunately the A38 at that time of the morning was busy enough to require Richard's basic concentration, so he approached the cottage, bathed in early morning light, still in one piece.

Three hours later he heard his wife's car coming up the lane. Three hours to think of all the things to say and do: tongue lashing, divorce, physical assault, acid attack or the ultimate in angst, murder.

A strange calm had overtaken Richard, because none of these would bring his career or his wife back. On the contrary, they would rob him of his bitterest revenge, humiliation.

"You're home early" said Claire, "nothing much on at the club or nothing much worth celebrating?"

Richard looked at his wife. He thought 'she knows there was no good news, but I'm buggered if I am going to give her the satisfaction of admitting it'. So carefully choosing his words he said: "I will have to wait for written orders regarding my future. Did you have a good evening?"

Claire grimaced and said: "You know how it is, I stayed over with Glennis Morgan after a few drinks. Her husband's away at sea".

Dejectedly, Richard muttered: "I guess that speaks for all of us."

Chapter 4

"Commander Nelson to see you."

Richard was ushered into the office of his solicitor by a lady who seemed older than the nineteenth century office that his lawyer occupied in the centre of Tavistock.

Adrian Pendleton rose to his feet and started to say: "Good to see you my old...chum", but his welcome words drifted away as he said: "Good God Richard, you look terrible. Are you sure you shouldn't be with a Doctor?"

Grey, dejected and defeated Richard sank into the visitor's chair opposite his oldest school friend and said: "I've come to change my will."

"I'm hazarding a guess, and to institute divorce proceedings?"

Richard stared at his friend and whispered "I can't believe this, you've known and never said anything". His voice rose. "You and who else? All my friends? Laughing behind my back. You bastard! You absolute bastard!"

Adrian held his hands up and peered through his round spectacles.

"No one really knew Richard; it was surmise and speculation that the 'perfect' couple were drifting apart.

People love scandal and titillation so what better than a loving husband at sea being cuckolded by his boss. But no one knew for sure, so call me what you will, I was not the one to spread a rumour that could have been purely the jealous envy of people who have nothing to enjoy in their own lives and could have easily ruined yours."

"Well, it doesn't really matter. There's nothing really of any value. The house is in our joint names, my few personal possessions can be collected and sent to my parents, and I've cleaned our building society account."

"Oh, can I ask why? It won't help in front of a divorce judge that you've nicked the family silver."

Richard's face was a mask as he said: "Don't worry it was silver already tarnished and I can think of better things to do with it."

As he left, Adrian clapped his arms round his shoulders and said: "Please Richard, come through this."

"I will, trust me. Can you recommend a local private detective to make a few inquiries for me?"

Chapter 5

The Brown Bear is a Devonport pub that many would say, when Plymouth was blitzed to pieces in WW2, survived more by luck than judgement.

In a small, smoke stained backroom bar Lt. Commander Colin McAndrew sat gloomily listening to his commanding officer describe the imminent end to all their ambitions and equally significantly, incomes and pension prospects.

Richard ended his narration of the meeting in London and sat nursing his pint. McAndrew moved his beer mat round the table, finally catching his friend's eyes.

"So what aren't you telling me? Frankly you look like a bag of shit. Ok, it's bad news, disastrous maybe, but nothing your crew will blame you for. Indeed, you put your neck on the line to stand up for me and them, so give old buddy, because if you want to pull rank and tell me to sod off I'll go now, and all our years together will be history."

Richard shifted awkwardly on the wooden bench.

"Right now I don't know whether I can even talk coherently about what has happened to my life. But we are due to go to sea shortly and if I can't cope you may find yourself in command."

"Jesus Christ Richard, you must be mad to tell me this. Are you really telling your first officer that he is going to sea with a potential psycho?"

"Well, you asked, and if I don't talk to someone soon I will go mad anyway."

The story was not long in telling and by the stony silence Richard knew that his friend at least had not been aware of the innuendo and rumours surrounding his marriage.

After a silence that seemed to last forever, McAndrew leaned forward and took Richards hand.

"You cannot know how devastated I am for you. We all know shit happens but this is shit beyond shit. God knows how you are coping, but one thing is certain, you and I will see our last and final tour through together. We will never give the bastard the satisfaction of not completing an A1 decommissioning cruise."

Richard brought another pint over and said: "What you've heard is my agony aunt story but what I am about to tell say is so unbelievably outrageous that you will probably call the men in white coats, and you will be in command of the last mission anyway."

Half an hour later, Colin McAndrew realised that even if life in prison awaited him, there was no way he could not be part of this extraordinary scheme.

Two days later twenty of the ninety-eight crew of HMS Torch were gathered in a private room rented by their CO in the Moorland Links Golf Club outside Tavistock.

"Gentlemen, thank you all for coming, and I thank Colin especially for taking it on himself to invite you to an unspecified but probably intriguing meeting. None of you will be old enough to remember an iconic film called the 'Dirty Dozen' starring a renegade US army officer charged with recruiting volunteers for a seemingly impossible mission. Some of you may even have seen a black comedy called 'The Italian Job' starring Michael Caine.

When I have finished what I have to say Colin and I will leave the room, so that any of you can go without any embarrassment or loss of face. All we can ask is you keep this a secret until whatever is achieved is a success or failure."

Colin McAndrew took the stage first and outlined the draconian terms of the redundancy package and especially Admiral Cruikshank's total unsympathetic response to being asked to offer a second chance for reenlistment or reposting.

When Richard Nelson concluded his own personal experience with his senior officers' behaviour, the atmosphere in the room was tangibly mutinous.

They listened to Richard's plan in stunned silence. Fifteen minutes later, both men returned to be greeted by twenty rigidly saluting crew members whose spokesman Able Seaman Finch simply said: "It didn't take five minutes for us to want to join up for the heist and reward of a lifetime"

Two stood and said prison sentences were more likely and with young families, could they be excused. But on their honour nothing would pass their lips until it was over.

Chapter 6

The Queen Victoria is the latest and most prestigious newcomer to the Cunard Fleet. Although Cunard is part of the Carnival group of cruise liner companies it retains all the Britishness of the glorious tradition of the 'Queens'.

Sailing from Southampton is a regular start to cruises worldwide and is an opportunity to victual with essential 'British' groceries: Angus beef, Welsh lamb, Cheddar and Stilton cheeses, even Aunt Bessie's Yorkshire Puddings – all make their way down the M3 or A34 to Southampton docks.

Scotney services on the A34 coming south from Newbury, is a welcome rest stop for many drivers before joining the M3 and M271 on the last run into dock gate 14. This windy, rain-swept morning is a typical working day for Bert Thomas as he sprints from his cab into the welcome warmth of the drivers' cafe. There is the usual banter amongst these knights of the road, and any thoughts of taking his tea and sandwiches back to the lorry are soon forgotten as a couple of obviously new HGV drivers engage him in conversation about his experiences, and never before asked for tips about favourite rest stops and tackling more than usual difficult road conditions.

Outside in the lorry park a small van parked beside Bert's Pantechnicon elicits little interest as the men in white overalls surreptitiously pick the lock, unload several packing cases and replace them with cartons all stamped with the 'Loch Fine Salmon' trademarks.

A security guard does finally inquire what they are doing and is reassured that the replacement is due to a last minute health warning about the salmon part of the consignment. Salmonella on a cruise liner is a nightmare for the owners, crew and passengers and a field day for the lawyers.

"My God I've been talking to you guys for over half an hour. Many thanks for the tea and good luck on the road."

The Trojan Horse never looked a bit like a forty ton articulated freezer truck with Eddie Stobart plastered down the side.

Since 1926 Kent and Curwen have been renowned for producing gentlemen's attire. The company has the privilege of dressing many of the most elegant sporting gentlemen in the world as suppliers of strip for Oxford University Boat Club, Wimbledon Tennis Championships and the official English Cricket Team clothiers. In 1930 Kent and Curwen introduced the iconic cricket sweater in white or cream with the distinctive striped V neck, which became a true classic of gentlemen's fashion.

Little surprise that the request for a complete cricket team outfit for 16 players and officials was a welcome order towards the end of the season. This late in the day, it was also no surprise that delivery was expected within two weeks. The cheque for £7,500 which accompanied the order added extra impetus for prompt manufacture.

Chapter 7

The weather on the morning Her Majesty's nuclear submarine HMS Torch finally left Devonport dock seemed to reflect the dismal end to a long hardworking but probably in Naval annals, uneventful career.

There was in the yard a sympathetic glance as the sub slipped its mooring and slowly moved past East Vanguard buoy into Plymouth Sound. There was no official send off, and there would certainly be no welcoming band on her return. This almost embarrassing indifference was welcomed by Commander Richard Nelson, who was sailing with a crew of eighty-two, not the regulation minimum personnel of ninety-eight. It was to be a routine Atlantic patrol so watches would be manned with fewer than usual, but the crew already had a suspicion that this was not a typical exercise.

The klaxon reverberated round the sub before the Commander opened his pre-op speech.

"Gentlemen, you no doubt are already guessing that this is a especially different patrol. It is, and I would ask you to be patient for a little while longer until we are further into it. Rest assured Lt. Commander Colin McAndrew and I will brief you fully as soon as we are able. God save the Queen."

But it wasn't Her Royal Highness that was uppermost in Richard's mind as he spoke. The Queen he was about to save was majestically moving down Southampton water with 2500 crew and 3500 passengers. Out into the Solent, the Sail Away party was in full swing and the members of the Tavistock Cricket Club 'on tour' were thoroughly enjoying themselves.

None of the lads noticed Petty Officer Simon Barnes, a good looking but normally shy and retiring youngster dallying with a stunning blonde in a tight-fitting revealing trouser suit.

"Dressed like that you certainly know how to bowl a maiden over."

With unaccustomed bravado, Barnes replied "Well, I'm always trying to improve my score."

Emily Robinson gave him a curious look and said: "Well anyway, perhaps we should send the silly mid off."

"Good idea" said Simon, thinking the less competition the better vying for the attention of this gorgeous girl.

"He was pretty stupid if you ask me."

Emily looked up at him, said: "I don't know what you're up to, but you know as little about cricket as my little finger. So you young Sir and your chums are stuck with me till I find out. I'm here as a guest passenger working for The Daily Telegraph as a travel correspondent. So take me to your leader and I'll join the team."

None of the passengers looked close enough to read the club motto on their immaculately tailored blazer pockets: 'Semper in excreta, solum profundum variat'. It was obvious that whilst sixteen single men sharing cabins might have raised a few eyebrows, a group of well-presented sportsmen, fellow players in a cricket team, did not.

The following day they participated fully in all the ship's entertainment programmes and were especially attentive during the bridge visit when the captain and several officers explained the miracles of the ship's navigation and communication systems. They were told that for safety reasons, visiting the engine rooms was prohibited but mobile phones could be used throughout the voyage but only at a hefty tariff.

The first port of call Madeira is approximately 1484 miles from Southampton (1800 nautical miles). Queen Victoria cruises at approximately 20 knots 480 nautical miles per day, in good weather 3-4 days across a slow, rolling Atlantic sea. Perfect for a bit of sunbathing and piracy.

There is always a time of day, particularly at night, when for a moment human activity seems to almost stop. It's the time for deepest sleep after the partying is over and the least alertness by those forced to work their shift.

Donning black outfits the sixteen cricket players and one with a slightly more shapely figure move out of their cabins. Stealthily, they slip through the ship without alarming the few cabin staff cleaning public corridors and rest areas. Several of them reach the galley area and a plastic toy machine rifle, which came abound in pieces in their suitcases, is assembled. Lookalike ferocious panga machetes are handed out. The kitchen staff on duty did not know what hit them when six seemingly heavily armed men in balaclavas hurtled through the swing doors from the main superior-standard restaurant.

Quickly bound and taped they watched as the team made their way into the freezer store and emerged some ten minutes later with a range of automatic pistols, machine guns and grenades that could arm a small army. They were distributed amongst the full group of sixteen men that assembled in the galley.

They all put on balaclavas, more to heighten the terror effect, as they all knew that since the sail away party; they were all on the CCTV system.

Without an unnecessary word or command they spread throughout the ship to their allotted tasks, the most important being: the engine room, the radio shack and the bridge. Having been repeatedly drilled with instructions that no resistance which could result in death or injury should be attempted in the event of a terrorist attack, the crew offered no resistance. The Captain Master Theodore Hamilton-Smythe was ordered to the bridge and told that his ship was now under the command of The Tavistock Cricket Team and to issue orders throughout the crews quarters that they should go about their normal duties, although they may notice that the ship itself was hove to.

"You won't get away with this" is probably one of the most overemployed phrases uttered by hostages and Hamilton-Smythe's bluster was met by scornful silence by the raiders on the bridge.

"Shut the fuck up, obey our orders and no one will get hurt or lose their shirt", said the bridge leader.

In the radio shack the young officer was already transmitting a demand for the equivalent of £20 million ransom for the ship, to be flown in by helicopter, in mixed cash currencies of dollars, sterling and euros.

In the engine room pipes connecting engine cooling systems to the sea were being disconnected and water started gushing in from the Atlantic. The massive bilge pumps were automatically activated which just about balanced the inflow of water.

In London the overnight administrative staff which ensured 24 hour, 365 day coverage for all the ships in the Cunard fleet, received the demand with shock, horror and incredulity. Urgent calls were made to all the board members and senior land-based sailing officers.

Masters with years of experience on cruise liners but actually floundering when they read the simple ransom demand.

"We are in total control of the liner Queen Victoria. The engine room flooding is being contained by the pumps. There is no risk of harm to passengers and crew providing a cash sum of £20 million in dollars, sterling and euros is landed by helicopter within 12 hours. Failure will result in the irretrievable sinking of the ship. You may remember the fate of the Holiday Magic only recently. We were responsible for the disaster, so do not attempt to play games or try any delaying tactics. We repeat, we are not interested in harming your ship, but only a small reward for handing her back to you still afloat."

Less than three hours after the takeover, the Captain made a statement over the ships PS system.

"Ladies and gentlemen, this is your captain. Since the early hours of this morning the Queen Victoria has been hijacked by a group of armed men claiming not to be terrorists but thieves, simply interested in a ransom demand for not sinking the ship. This has been communicated to our head office in London. Although like all my officers, I am under their control, they seem to be reasonable, rational and entirely clinical about their mission. For this reason they have directed me to reassure you that they intend no harm to crew or passengers and ask you to continue to enjoy your day. Please do not attempt any independent action that will jeopardise the safety of the ship. Thank you from your Captain for listening."

As the multiple breakfast restaurants filled up, comparisons were voiced about any cruise ship disaster story they could think of. Andre Doria, Titanic, Costa Concordia, Poseidon Adventure and ships taken by the Somali pirates like Seaborn Spirit where the owners paid a ransom of £1.5 million out of a total of £29.2 million ransom monies surrendered in 2012.

Inevitably small groups of self-opinionated ex-military 'experts' got together to argue over the feasibility of recapturing the ship but the sheer scale of the ship's size made any realistic plan impractical, and fraught with the risk of sending her to the bottom sooner rather than later.

In 1985, four Palestinian terrorist boarded the Italian cruise liner 'Achille Lauro' shortly after if left Alexandria, Egypt. They demanded the release of PCF members but when Syria denied port entry they shot a US wheelchair-bound passenger, 69yr old Leon Klinghoffer and threw him overboard.

They did a deal to leave the ship in Egypt but their plane en route to Libya was forced down by US F14 jets to land in Italy. They received various prison sentences and their leader Abbas was finally captured and died in American custody in 2004.

Chapter 8

Out in the Atlantic, some three hundred metres below the surface, HMS Torch was preparing to send up her radio mast for the mornings flash message from the admiralty with latest orders and other relevant information regarding her patrol.

Colin McAndrew received the micro-second message transcribed by the radio officer and went into the captain's cuddy which served as his office and berth. He always found it difficult to address his best friend by rank, but this morning he felt a duty to give Richard Nelson his full naval title.

"Commander, it is my duty to inform you that a British cruise liner, the Queen Victoria has been hijacked for ransom by an as yet unknown group of armed men. We are ordered to proceed directly to her position and stand by to render any possible assistance."

Richard stood and with a grin a mile wide on his face, clapped his friend round the shoulders and said "Lt. Commander, I suggest you send an immediate confirmation and set course immediately for the designated rendezvous.

"Oh my God, what a piece of poetic justice. You couldn't believe it if you read it in a book!" spluttered Richard Nelson.

"Well you have to admit, being ordered to become game keeper instead of poacher is a turn up for the books. I'll send a reply straight away. Incidentally Sir, it might be slightly difficult to change course as we are already on it, but what the hell!"

With a farewell grin Colin McAndrew disappeared off into the bowels of the submarine.

Cunard's insurers, a Lloyds consortium, gathered in the Cunard Directors boardroom and joined the discussion as to how to respond to the ransom demand.

"Let's start with the basic question", said the weasily lead counsel for the insurers. "Here we have a £450 million ship, state of the art technology, and yet a handful of guys take it over and threaten to sink it, period. Surely this cannot be practically possible. There must be overriding safety features that can prevent this happening?"

Maurice Foster, the Managing Director of the Cunard line, said, once the hub bub of agreement had died down: "Regretfully, I can tell you, period, that the 'guys' have already proved their point once. Assuming of course they use the same guys, but I'm not going to assume they are not. They know ships and we have made contact with the Chief Engineer on board, kind courtesy of these guys as you call them. He has confirmed that water is pouring into Queen Victoria via the disconnected sea cooling engine pipes. The pumps are coping but only just. Disconnect a few more pipes and blow up the bilge pump generators and the ship will sink, period."

"So you simply suggest we lie on our backs, have out tummies tickled and pay up?" This from another insurer.

"Frankly £20 million for a £450 million investment sounds quite cheap to me."

John Aitken the deputy finance director muttered.

"Where are the SAS, the paras, the special boat squadron?" queried another insurer.

"Don't be ridiculous" snapped the Cunard safety specialist, "We are talking about a ship some 200 miles offshore, in nearly half a mile depth of water, leaking like a sieve, in the hands of a gang of well-armed hijackers who will scuttle the boat the moment any threat looms over the horizon."

"Let's look at the worst scenario", this from Cunard's Chairman, Lloyd Thomas.

"The ship sinks, £450 million down the pan, 3500 passengers take to lifeboats and sue – another £35 million? Lawyers costs another 10% £45 million. We are staring at £500 million or more in the face. I suggest we take a vote because time is running out and I'm not betting against the bank that these guys have an exit plan that enables them to walk or swim, whatever we decide.

And even if we decide to send them marked notes, I suspect they are clever enough that we would be tracking them all around the globe forever and never catch up."

With one abstention and one predictable vote against, it is agreed that the money will be collected and despatched post haste by long range helicopter.

In the Ministry of Defence, a hastily summoned emergency committee is also debating what action could be taken.

"A frontal seaborne rescue operation would be domed because the ship's hugely sensitive radar would detect any untoward activity from 35 miles away or more. In any case, once spotted, blowing the pipes and bilge pumps would guarantee we could never repair them in time. They could in the meantime herd a thousand or more hostages into the theatre, and we would be powerless!"

The SAS and Special Boat officers concurred that any attempt to land from the air would be similarly doomed.

"What about our nuclear sub in the area?"

"It's been sent there to monitor the situation" said Admiral Cruikshank, "not to sink the bloody ship".

"So what do we tell the PM?" asked the Chairman of the Chiefs of Staff. Answering his own question he said bluntly: "cough up, claim on the insurance and recruit these men as security advisors against future hostages of fortune!"

"If no one has any better suggestion I'm phoning the PM right now."

The silence round the conference table said it all.

"So that's it," exploded the Prime Minister, Martin Roberts, "No point in calling a COBRA meeting because we've already given in. And you are expecting me to bat for an increase in the armed forces budget next year. The best equipped forces in the world and powerless against a small gang of robbers!"

"You can have my resignation now if you wish Prime Minister, but I cannot and will not sacrifice life just to appease political vanity."

"Ok, Ok, point taken, just don't include this conversation in your memoirs when they are written" replied the PM acidly.

"Anyway have we got a helicopter suitable?" asked the PM.

"I'm chartering a Dauphin AS365 which has a range of nearly 500 nautical miles and will carry £20 million quite easily. They can refuel on-board if a return trip is necessary, and can bring back our crooks in superb comfort if they wish".

"You don't seem to be taking this very seriously" said the PM testily.

"On the contrary Prime Minister, I've always enjoyed cruise liner holidays, but I'm afraid that this affair might just put the wife off."

They both slammed the phone down at the same moment.

The Commissioner of the Met Police presided over an equally cobbled together emergency meeting with senior Special Branch M15 and M16 officers.

"So we know absolutely nothing about this group except they were able to board the ship fully armed without detection and claim to be able to leave with impunity."

The senior Special Branch officer Jordan Leech said: "In a nutshell, yes. Furthermore there is no sighting of them via satellite surveillance as they have absolutely no need to go on deck."

"Well, whoever they are I hold my hat off to them" said the M16 security chief responsible for UK domestic spy catching. "This could be the crime of the century."

"You may be right" said the Metropolitan Police Commissioner, unfolding a note bought into the room. "I am now told that Cunard, after receiving advice from our military chiefs of staff, have confirmed that the ransom will be paid without delay.

"But they still have to escape with the dosh?" queried one aide.

"Well, the helicopter being used is capable of 145kts and 12 passengers plus payload so they can easily return to the Portuguese coastline in any place they choose. Even if they are monitored by satellite they can still duck and dodge military and police flexible response to round them up as they land. If they are as well organised as they appear to be, I don't doubt that they've thought this through and come up with an answer that frankly may amaze us."

The M15 officer grinned and said: "so far no injuries, no deaths, this could be the Italian Job of the 21st Century. I wonder when the bus will come off the road."

Chapter 9

"Murder of civilians regardless of their crime is not in the remit of Her Majesty's navy." The Royal Navy spokesman was responding to a question by journalists, now the fate of the liner was revealed.

"The job of identifying and arresting those accused is the responsibility of the criminal authorities. If the helicopter carrying the money and the hijackers leave the ship, our submarines and naval surface ships will not bring it down by rocket or gunfire."

Commander Richard Nelson turned to his first officer and said: "Well, that is one weight off our shoulders, although it is actually quite clearly laid down in our rules of engagement that we are not part of the civilian police force."

On board the Queen Victoria the reaction amongst the hijackers that their demands were being met was received with a calm detachment that somewhat mystified the bridge officers. They were bound but not gagged, and relieved at the news that unless anything untoward happened they would be on their way to Madeira within approximately six hours.

As evening fell, the bars and restaurants filled up with excited passengers looking forward to continuing their holiday but with what a tale to tell!

Meanwhile water continued to flood into the ship's bilges. The Chief Engineer under guard was allowed to make regular checks that the generators serving the pumps, and the pumps themselves, were coping adequately.

However, his next report to the Captain was more alarming: "Generator 2 and pump 3 are overheating. They were not designed to run at maximum overload capacity for so long. For God's sake, land the cash!"

"Flood the helicopter deck!" instructed the hijacker to one of the ships electricians. Faintly out of the night sky the familiar whop whop whop sound of an approaching helicopter could be heard.

After checking the contents as best they could of the 10 metal containers jammed full with money, the helicopter was refuelled.

Radio contact was maintained with the pilot from the ship's communication centre. Landing coordinates were given on a remote area of Portuguese coast. At the very last minute, one of his 'guests' would give him new coordinates and this would be his landing site. Shore based receivers would detect any deviation from this plan and the fate of the ship would be his damoclean sword for life.

Approximately 45 minutes after landing 12 figures dressed in black with balaclava helmets carried 10 metal cases to the helicopter. Viewed with night vision thermal imaging the watchers, from a ship on the horizon, saw the departure of the 'copter with scepticism. "This is too easy for us to track" observed one viewer.

"Maybe the Italian Job bus" said another.

They were not surprised to hear a flash message from the hijackers that they still retained control of the ship and only when they heard the ransom money was safely ashore would they leave peacefully.

"How?" grunted one officer aboard a navy ship over the horizon. "Beam me up, Scotty?"

"Well if the money disappears and we manage to arrest to arrest those left, they'll receive 20 years max a piece and be out in 10. Not a bad reward as long as they can trust their mates."

"They could surely never risk that, even if they were all in the same family", Captain Rule replied. "My bet is a very very fast offshore speedboat, alongside and gone at 60 knots or more. The drug runners between Cuba and the USA have the most amazing craft that can outrun virtually anything even the American coastguard possesses.

After dark and with instructions that we are not authorised to shoot to kill or injure they will be away before we can even react. Don't forget we are actually less than 160 miles from the Portuguese coast. They could be there in 2 hours. For £20 million, ditching a £300,000 boat is chickenfeed."

Two and a half hours later 12 bemused retired holidaymakers from the Queen Victoria wandered into the local police station near Oporto and ask for a bed for the night.

Chapter 10

There is no moon tonight; even the stars have remained unlit. The sea slops gently against the hull of the massive ship, brightly lit like London's Regent Street in the weeks leading up to Christmas.

Waiters pushing trollies through the ships corridors, descending in lifts, pushing past inebriated passengers attract no attention.

For safety reasons the reception area, beside the doors in the side of the ship that allow passengers to disembark in the ships lifeboats to visit ports of call where her draught is too deep to allow harbour entry, is cordoned off.

Twelve waiters swiftly remove their white uniforms and open the watertight doors. Although it may seem old hat in this technological age, a few powerful torchlight flashes is all that is needed to being two black rubber inflatables alongside. The bags concealed in the trolleys are quickly loaded and in a rush, the other four waiters arrive.

Unnoticed, the inflatables speed away, the engine noise specially muffled for clandestine operations, although the Navy probably hadn't quite imagined them being used for this type of jaunt.

Alongside HMS Torch the luggage and occupants of the boats were soon hustled below, and a few knife thrusts sent the dinghies to Davy Jones locker. Even if the conning tower had been a radar target for other ships in the locality, its appearance was so brief that it was easily dismissed as a radar blip of no consequence.

"Who the hell are you?"

Before she could reply, PO Simon Barnes said: "It's all my fault Sir, I let the side down big time. But Emily here has joined up, hopefully one day to tell the story of a lifetime."

"Don't worry about me, Captain" said Emily, "I'll keep out of your way. But let me help you in my own profession to get your own back on the sickening way you and your men have been treated."

"Gentlemen, this is your Captain. And time to briefly update you with our mission's progress. We have, with the dedication and skill of a small group of our officers and men, succeeded so far in bringing off an extraordinary feat that will never be forgotten in the history of the Royal Navy. I cannot yet tell you what we have achieved but I will tell you why you will be able to hold your head up high when you can say 'I was there'. On our return to port, this submarine and all of its officers and crew, yes you and I, will be made redundant. We are to be given minimum pension rights and severance pay. This voyage will at least enable us to demonstrate that the qualities of skill, ingenuity and determination that once made the Royal Navy the best in the world still exists in its sailors.

We have successfully stolen £20 million, a fitting recompense for your lost jobs, salaries and pensions.

We will disembark in our No.1's so polish your boots till they gleam! God save the Queen."

Aboard the Queen Victoria the bridge crew gradually realise that the hijackers are nowhere in sight. After thirty minutes, the navigation officer is the first to free his wrists. The sense of relief that they are free and unharmed is shadowed by the fear that elsewhere in the ship some greater disaster has befallen the passengers or crew.

The reality of hearing about the £20 million ransom, and the urgency of implementing engineering repairs soon bring them down to earth. With patched up pumps and generators, the Queen Victoria slowly sails to Madeira with a chastened Captain pondering to anyone listening if there was anything that he or anyone else could have done to have averted this humiliating near catastrophe.

Chapter 11

"Message from the Admiralty Sir, terminate surveillance of Queen Victoria, shorten patrol and return to Devonport by 17.00 hours Sunday 3rd October."

"Looks like Monday the 4th is going to be a busy day", stated Colin McAndrew, "What with our redundancy cheques and all that."

Ignoring his friend's jibe Commander Nelson and Emily concentrated on writing signals for transmission to their contacts ashore.

Without a welcome ceremony, HMS Torch berths silently alongside Devonport dockyard at precisely 17.00 hours and the crew begin to pack their personal kit for their final disembarkation to 'blighty'. The crews' quarters soon resonate to the sound of shoe brushes and the sweet aroma of kiwi parade ground polish

Two specially chartered National Express 56 seater coaches greet the crew at 7am on a grey, misty October morning. They soon swallow the immaculately dressed 98 (and 1 girl) matelots and move steadily through Devonport to the A38, joining the M5 at Exeter and the M4 at the Bristol interchange.

Five hours later the buses are parked in Horse Guards Avenue. A passing traffic warden is too confused to think about issuing a ticket when a pristine squad of naval officers and ranks form up and march up Horse Guards Avenue, past the lone statue of a Ghurkha, to the MOD Main Building, as it's known, Whitehall.

Passers-by are urged on by police trying to keep the roads and pavements free for passing traffic. Their task is made more difficult by the media circus gathered outside the main entrance. Cameramen jostle newspaper reporters, TV and radio interviewers push and shove for front row positions.

"You knew this was going to happen" accused the Deputy Chief Commissioner of Police for London.

"There are insufficient police officers to control this unseemly fracas and yet you seem unconcerned as if you are actually condoning this 'scrum'".

His boss grinned and said "I'm not concerned, so sit back and enjoy the show."

"Troop, Shun!" shouted the lead Lieutenant. 98 men crashed to attention; only those at the rear pulling 10 trolleys were slightly less than perfect.

"Commander Richard Nelson, Royal Navy HMS Torch to see Admiral Cruikshank", announced the same Lieutenant to a bemused doorman.

"Do you have an appointment?" queried the official.

"Do we look as though we need an appointment?" replies the officer.

"No, I suppose not, hang on a mo and I'll see what I can do."

"Do that, we'll wait!"

"I'll have his balls for breakfast!" spluttered Cruikshank, "You already have Sir" replied his aide de camp, "you've fired him already so if I may respectfully suggest Sir, further threats are pretty pointless."

"Don't be impertinent, just make yourself useful, and get my cap".

Emerging into bright sunlight, the Admiral was somewhat astounded by the gathering in front of him. Still, he thought, I am looking my best so a good photo-shoot opportunity can only improve my image with the powers that be.

Patting his hair down he donned his cap and returned the Commander's snappy salute.

"Commander, I imagine there is an adequate explanation for this quite extraordinary demonstration."

"Sir, in keeping with the Navy's highest tradition of military ingenuity and honour, the officers and crew of HMS Torch are proud to be able to return the £20 million ransom paid to rescue the Queen Victoria. Gentlemen, please bring forward the cases containing the cash. A final tribute from the men, who in a few days, by your orders, will leave the service they have dedicated their lives to".

The Admiral realised with alarm this was not quite the photo opportunity he was expecting.

Recovering quickly he said: "I am not here to discuss naval strategy with you Commander, but to offer thanks for your amazing success in recapturing the ransom".

Under his breath he whispered: "you bastard, you robbed it and now you're rubbing my nose in it. I will see you in hell for this".

Ignoring the Admiral's remarks, Commander Nelson stood back and said: "My second duty Sir is less palatable. The papers please, Adrian". Richard's solicitor handed him a sheaf of documents.

"These are the divorce affidavits naming you as the co-respondent who has shagged my wife during the past two years. A suggested letter of resignation is also included".

Dumbstruck the Admiral could only accept the proffered papers, and ashen-faced, about turned and almost ran back into the building.

The cacophony of sound amongst the gobsmacked journalists and onlookers was drowned out by a barked command

"Three cheers for the Commander! Hip Hip..." The three hoorays could probably be heard in Devonport where many of the wives and girlfriends of the crew had gathered in a Devonport pub tipped off by Richard's solicitor that they were about to witness 'a bit of a do'.

"About turn, quick march!" The coaches were soon swallowed up in London traffic. Everyone was keenly listening for sounds of sirens warning of imminent pursuit.

But even before they boarded the buses Richard's solicitor had his hand held up for silence.

"I have a statement to make and ask for a few moments attention. Commander Richard Nelson wants it to be clearly understood that today's meeting and the events that led up to it are entirely his responsibility. The naval code of discipline made any attempt to disobey the Captain's orders as an act of mutiny so his crew have to be entirely exonerated from any blame attached to their actions. The crew were told by the Commander that they were sitting on £20 million in unmarked cash, and they could elect to take any or all of it on return to Devonport. There was not one dissent to handing the entire amount back.

The interest this story will generate will play for some time to come. Richard and his crew have asked that all requests for interviews etcetera will be handled through my office, or" he paused and grinned as he said "or through the offices of the Crown Prosecution Service".

"So we do nothing?" queried the Assistant Commissioner.

"Not on my orders, we don't" his boss replied.

"The MOD building is within the boundaries of the MET police to be sure. But there is no harm to life or limb, there is no damage to goods or chattels that the insurers won't cover, and let <u>them</u> be brave enough to sue Richard Nelson. There is no robbery, so no case to answer. If the MOD wants to pursue it, let them. I think public opinion would laugh them out of court. Let's go and drink to the wonderful thought that the days of the swashbuckling hero are not yet over!"

Putting the last few personal possessions in to his battered briefcase, Commander Nelson looks up as two burly Royal Navy police appear at the entrance to his cabin.

"Come to arrest me at long last?"

"No Sir", replied the Senior Office, "But we must escort you off the boat. Signals have been received confirming your dishonourable discharge from the Navy. So will you come quietly or do we have to forcibly eject you?"

The officer laughed as he said: "You have no idea, Sir, how much the lads admire you. Can I shake your hand rather than manacle it?"

Without a backward glance Richard leaves the dockyard knowing that life without the Navy and his wife was a bitter reward for exacting a savage, humiliating revenge.

Epilogue

"The Ministry of Defence has announced today that Admiral Howard Cruikshank has, for personal reasons, resigned with immediate effect from the Royal Navy. Appreciation of his years of service has been offered by the Prime Minister, who did however say that in the circumstances the Admiral did the best thing for the honour of the Navy and his own reputation".

Claire Nelson stood in the small lounge of Burntwood Cottage as the TV presenter went on to other news. As a car pulled up the lane, she reached down to turn the set off.

Richard Nelson silently dragged himself through the front door.

"So you're still here" he observed casually.

"Why, where do you expect me to be? I still own half the cottage and until I find somewhere else to live I'm sorry but I'll be staying put.

"But I thought you would be..." Richard's voice tailed off as Claire looked at him with a rush of sympathy at his dejected and weary face.

"Ah, you mean why am I not ensconced in the arms of my lover? Well, it may not surprise you to know that my Lothario and dragon slayer has mysteriously disappeared below the waves. I've not been able to reach him by phone, text or email. Perhaps he's fallen on his sword".

"I wish" said Richard.

"Anyway, how was work?" Richard tried hard to keep any resentment out of his voice.

"Well, apart from a few cool glances and obvious words behind my back, frankly the hospital is so busy no one really has the time to think about anything other than the patients. Anyway broken relationships are the rule rather than the exception in most hospitals. How about you?"

Richard smiled wanly as he said: "Well believe it or not you are talking to the Man of the Moment. So far Adrian has received innumerable press and TV requests for interviews. I've been offered three jobs with international security firms, one with an insurance company and a sales managership with BMW in Plymouth. All the lads have been inundated with job offers, personal interviews and the like. Best of all though, which I really have to accept, is a year's contract with Cunard to lecture on board their fleet of liners. What a laugh!"

Except Richard wasn't laughing, he was staring at Claire with an unfathomable expression. Finally they both looked away. He idly flicked a bit of dust off the coffee table and finally said quietly: "It doesn't really matter. I mean, I'm not really cut out to be a gung-ho personality hero type".

He fidgeted again with another piece of dust and continued.

"In any case, you might well guess that without you in my life everything else is a crock of proverbial shit. So

I'll leave you to it as I don't think both of us can stay here."

"Oh Richard, I am so very, very sorry. What a complete and utter fucking mess I've made of our lives". Tears brimmed in Claire's eyes.

"Well" said Richard, "perhaps at least you've got time for a pie and pint down the pub".

"I may have, if you're paying" replied Claire, but giggled as she said: "Are you sure your head won't be too big to go through the door?"

As they walked down the lane Richard tentatively took Claire's hand to steer her past the potholes.

Sometimes even the rockiest road can be resurfaced.

The End

Chapter 1

Everyone loved Freddie Wharburton (with an 'h' you know! The ordinary, other Warburtons bake bread and cakes, so distressingly common). Not that Freddie was really a snob; it's just that he felt he was different from the other mere toilers in this life's mortal coil.

From the top of his pink (not too pink) bald head and the fluffy white curls that surrounded it, down to the Loakes brown suede brogue shoes, Freddie was every inch what he knew he was, a Thespian, an actor, dear boy! Noel Coward would have been proud of Freddie's impersonation, and his way of eating chocolates delicately with two fingers

The only slight fly in the ointment was that Freddie's life was a sham. From his earliest school days Freddie wanted to be on stage. He was up for every school play, volunteered for any drama part going. And he got them. Unfortunately, if it was 'Macbeth' he was never Macbeth or even Banquo or his ghost. Freddie would be one of the three witches or worse.

In short, poor Freddie was doomed to be one of the theatres 'extras', walk on parts, the occasional one liner. As a butler "I'll be leaving you now" was to be his destiny as a fully paid up member of Equity.

Nevertheless, after leaving school and a brief unmemorable spell at RADA, Freddie was still convinced that despite all the put downs his day would come, and he would be a STAR.

Of course, funding this ambition from day one proved to be a chore. One simply had to live in London, the centre of the known world of theatre waiting for the break to inevitably come. Camden Town wasn't quite Hampstead Hill, where the really successful Thespians lived but it was close enough. After all it was on the Northern line!

His one room studio apartment over Mr & Mrs Rajit Singhs' newsagents was a treasure trove of theatrical memorabilia, and certainly his original posters advertising 'Gandhi' had the authentic smell of curry, kind courtesy of the Landlord and his lady.

Freddie can't quite believe that his last birthday was his 60th. He lived alone for so long, that most dates apart from Christmas and New Year simply went unnoticed. But he still had his own teeth and what was left of his hair. And he was still relatively fit thanks to a regime of shelf-filling, dog walking and any other odd jobs that paid the rent.

As Freddie pointed out to anyone who would listen, being an actor meant you had to be available at the drop of a hat (or the raising of a curtain!) A proper serious career type job was completely out of the question. Part time was in, full time was out.

As part consequence of this erratic financial programme, Freddie had never married. Even marriage itself may have curtailed Freddie's freedom to rush off to the siren call of the stage. Still, he was not gay, no indeed. He may now be on the shelf at 60 but he had been taken down and dusted a few times! His soft liquid brown eyes, delicate turn of phrase and a lunch box that would be the envy of many of his fellow actors had kept his bed warm on many a night. Few returned however, complaining that the smell of curry permeating his apartment had lingered long after they had arrived at work the following morning. Being asked by your colleagues if you had changed your name to Edwina Currie did not bode well for a return visit.

The cruel winds of the economic downturn were flapping around Freddie's nightshirt, as some of his regular clients were forced to cut back. Out of work bankers wives were forced to walk their own dogs, the local Tescos and Iceland were increasingly hiring cheaper Russian and Polish labour. How could Freddie survive? A cheaper flat, impossible, he would have to go to a Salvation Army hostel. Give up the car? Never had one! Eat less? Do us a favour! The Singhs already subsidised his diet with surplus curries. New, alternative sources of income? Now you're talking, but where from?

Freddie is in his local hostelry downing a few pints with a few of his fellow would-be Thespians when a rather large flowery lady walked over and in a booming Chelsea Flower Show sort of voice said "you are Freddie Wharburton if I am not mistaken."

"Oh my God, it's Poppy 'Flower Pot' Wisteria" exclaimed Freddie.

"Well, actually Fred, its Deirdre Jones but I like the style so come and have a drink and tell me what you have been doing since you shagged me in that flat you seduced me back to claiming it was the Taj Mahal."

An hour later Freddie's head was reeling with a new found sense of opportunity and financial security.

Deirdre had come over from nearby St Johns Wood to interview a potential candidate and had spotted Freddie purely by chance through the window of the pub. Even if the aroma of eau de curry was long forgotten. Freddie's lunch-box was not. But more to the point Deirdre Jones, now owned one of the most successful child minding, nursery care and babysitting agencies in NW8. "The pay is £6.50 an hour and £12 an hour after 12 o'clock. The bookings are flexible and absolutely these days non-sexist. But I only employ carers with a qualification."

So day two Freddie is on his NVQ course in Camden College. Never had any children of his own, and too old to remember his own childhood, Freddie is somewhat overwhelmed when he discovers he has an absolute empathy with babies and youngsters. Top of the class, he returned with his new credentials to Deirdre who insists it's time to celebrate by reopening the lunch box (with some accompanying champagne of course).

Cycling over to NW8 on one of Boris's Bikes is now a regular part of Freddie's almost daily or rather evening agenda. Dressed in his finest Thespian outfits he cuts a very stylish figure as he rings the door bells to some of the wealthiest families in London. After all, most of his very, very elegant clothes were probably donated by several of his clients to the lovely charity shops that litter St Johns Wood High Street. Freddie can afford Turnbull and Asser shirts, Gucci loafers, Hugo Boss jackets and Gieves and Hawkes suits, kind courtesy of the kind people he is babysitting for. Not that they would say anything even if they recognised the clothes, because as Freddie would be the first to admit, much to his surprise, most of clients are genuinely such nice people.

Except the Vlassas.

It has become a regular booking, and only because of the late hours and hefty tip does Freddie agree to continue. No one quite knows how Gregory Vlassa came to London, what his business was before, and how much he is worth now. And no one who has met him would have the audacity to ask: East European, Ukrainian, Georgian, Russian or Romanian, he could be all of these. His minder, Gregor, could certainly be a Goth or Vandal from the Ural Mountains.

He has a wife, 5 years older who has followed him from eastern Europe and resigned to a back room in his lifestyle. The house is magnificent, probably one of the finest in north London. No expense has been spared by several of London's most exclusive and experienced interior designers to create the impression that Gregory Vlassa and his wife are people of impeccable taste and breeding. At first sight, and after initial introductions, many visitors are seduced by the overwhelming artistic opulence to think just that. The Provenance of some of his Masters oil paintings may be questionable but who cares after sampling the glories of his wine cellar. Berry Brothers and Rudd Wine Merchants in St James have almost dedicated a van and driver so regular do they deliver to his address.

For Gregory Vlassa is a man of big, exotic and erotic tastes. He is a big man standing over 6' 3" tall, his large frame bulges with the sort of muscle that personal fitness trainers dream about. His appetites are gargantuan, verging on gross, but his virile good looks and razor sharp intellect dominate whatever company he is entertaining, or more likely, subjugating, with the force of his views.

Gregory Vlassa's sexual conquests are equally varied and extreme, most much younger than his 50 years. Whilst he is not averse to paying for his more bizarre fetishes, he prefers his conquests to be fiercely independent and consensual with the energy and imagination they both put into their sexual coupling. His latest tiger is 26 years of age and works for him as a sort of girl Friday. Officially she works as a journalist for one of the newspapers that Vlassa now owns. But she will undertake any of Vlassa's demands as she is disgusted enough with herself to realise that she is obsessed with Vlassa, his brain and his body. Trisha Ellson (don't make jokes about me going down the pan!) knows that she is besotted by a megalomaniac thug who will crush anything and anyone that stands in his way.

Meeting Alexandra Vlassa for the first time two years ago, Trisha knew that Alexi as she preferred to be called, recognised another notch on the bedpost of her husband's love affairs. Describing Alexi once Sunday lunchtime when, for a while she stepped back to the real world of her loving caring parents in their modest semi in Croydon, she said, "She is one of the loveliest women I have ever met. Nothing seems to faze her, she treats her husband like an over indulged pet and seems to float along on a cloud of her own. Her two Labradors with the biggest brown eyes you have ever seen are the closest she comes to normality in this evil house."

"Why do you say evil?" Trisha's mothers mind is already working overtime to calculate if her beloved daughter is at risk from this strange household.

"Well, nothing is ever really without a sense of underlying violence. The twins for example, are given almost free rein to do what they like. Consequently they are always pushing their behaviour to the limit. They are like sugar and cream with their father who idolises them but they are utterly horrible to anyone else, especially the staff in the house. I don't even think they especially respect or even love their mother, Alexi, as they often speak to her as if she's a senile incompetent. Oh well mum, he pays well and I don't have to live there."

But even as she spoke Trisha could not forget the last time she and Gregory had sex in his office. On the floor, over the desk, torn clothes, sexual frenzy for nearly an hour, every orifice surrendered and plundered. There would be a next time and a time again. The journey was hateful and degrading but irresistible.

Chapter 2

Although Freddie has never met Trisha Ellson, he would have roundly applauded her overview of the Vlassa household. There was nothing he could specifically put his finger on but he always felt a tinge of unease when he entered Manoir House. It certainly never helped when Gregor was around, his permanent scowl and large bulge under his left armpit gave Freddie the creeps. Even in his naivety Freddie knew Gregor was 'packing'. The only person Freddie did feel sort of comfortable with was Alexi but Freddie rarely had more than a few words with her, fearing it might somehow upset Gregory. Even more unnerving, perhaps, were the twins themselves, nine years of age going on nineteen, they were beautiful, precocious and coldly indifferent. No amount of attempted conversation or good humour had ever thawed their dismissive attitude to Freddie. So a long time ago he had given up trying. 'Take the money and run' was how he summed it up, if asked why he put up with their evident hostility.

Three o'clock on a miserable Tuesday afternoon, Freddie is cleaning his flat. A chore not undertaken lightly as he cherishes every photo, programme and prop that owes any relationship to his acting career. Shortly after 3:30 his mobile phone rings with its strident rendering of the overture which accompanies the dance routine from Folies Bergere.

"Freddie is that you?" Deirdre Jones continues without waiting for a reply.

"I need you to help me out. Gregory Vlassa has asked for a minder tonight at very short notice, mentioned you and said he would pay an extra bonus. Please don't let me down."

Ever stuck for cash and his mobile phone bill due, Freddie reluctantly agreed to help out.

"Be there at 6.30pm as they must be away by 6:45pm. It could be a late one: one to one-thirty or so, but I know you'll cope."

With her usual throaty laugh Deirdre rings off.

Cycling over and hoping his batteries will last long enough to keep the lamps going on his return, Freddie chains the bike to the iron railing by the front door.

"I wish you wouldn't do that," is Gregory Vlassa's opening remark, "It scratches the paintwork and I do have electric security gates."

"Sorry" says Freddie already wrong footed, "Force of habit I suppose."

"Anyway, come in and get settled quickly as we're off."

Inside the house the usual visceral atmosphere feels even worse than normal. Ever sensitive to the nuances of strained human relationships, Freddie senses that there has been a real ruck going on before he had arrived.

"I'm afraid the twins are being very difficult" Alexi says joining them, dressed to kill in a flowing red evening dress.

"But Gregory had this very important dinner and theatre date thrust upon him at the last moment and the clients are too important to refuse. The twins had hoped we were taking them out for supper.

Gregory chimed in: "Well, don't take any nonsense from them, and be absolutely certain they go to bed by 8 o'clock as they have important exams tomorrow which count towards their next public school entry, so I don't want them to fuck up."

In his full chauffeur's regalia, Gregor opens the front door and ushers them down to the Mercedes 600 limo waiting in the drive.

Freddie wanders into the main lounge where the biggest TV set you can buy is located. The twins are sat watching a cartoon programme but as soon as Freddie appears they pointedly turn the set off and, apart from looks that could freeze hell over, walk out slamming the door with force enough to make glasses in the cocktail cabinet rattle.

Settling himself down with a tray of sandwiches and bottle of wine from the fridge kindly left by Alexi, Freddie tunes into channel 4 news at 7 o'clock. When it's over it will be time enough to get the children to bed.

World War 3 and the Cold War combined could not have prepared Freddie for the vicious mouth slapping that the twins responded to his announcement that it was time for bed. So joined at the hip were they that their insults were almost spoken in unison.

"You slimy little shit, we'll get you back don't worry."

Shaken, but unhurt, Freddie resumes his TV evening until just after one, when the Vlassa's return and give Freddie a very generous reward for an evening when he genuinely thinks he's really earned it.

Chapter 3

Two days later, Freddie is incarcerated in his bedsit by a heavy cold and pouring rain. Wondering who would be buzzing his entry phone at three in the afternoon, he is surprised to be speaking to Chief Detective Inspector Ian Brown who asks if it would be convenient for he and Mandy Phillips to come up. Quickly removing his cleaning pinafore and washing his hands, he greets them at the door with a smile. They apologise for dripping over his floor, but their glances at his threadbare carpet remind Freddie that he hasn't a lot to show for 60 years of living.

"You are Fredrick Wharburton?" asks the Inspector.

"I am, because as you can see by my home, it wouldn't pay anyone to impersonate me" quips Freddie.

"Quite so Mr Wharburton, but just to confirm who we are, here are our warrant cards."

Freddie inspects the proffered cards and asks if they would like some tea. Only Mandy accepts and accompanies him into the alcove that serves as a kitchen. The Inspector takes the opportunity to give the room a once over, spotting the ancient Dell laptop on the table that serves as a desk, dining table and ironing board.

Once they are seated the Inspector starts by asking personal questions about Freddie's age, how long he's lived there and what work he does.

Although he is mystified by this interest in his personal details, Freddie can't quite grasp the purpose of this visit and says so.

"Can you please tell us Mr Wharburton where you were on the evening of the 6th September?"

"Certainly, I was child minding at the Vlassa's from early evening"

"How can you be so certain?"

"Well, to start with, it was only two evenings ago and probably one of the most unpleasant I've had in a long while."

"Unpleasant?" asks Mandy Philips, "Can you describe the evening for us?"

Dimly Freddie is aware that this might be more serious than he thought, but proceeds to give a full account of the night including the hostile behaviour of the twins towards him.

"So you don't remember going upstairs to Tania Vlassa's bedroom after they had gone to bed?"

"Certainly not, I have no reason to supervise them upstairs as they not babies but 9 year old youngsters."

"Inspector, I don't want to appear obstructive but is there a point to your questions?"

"Well yes there is sir. Can you also confirm whether you saw Toby Vlassa after he went to bed."

"I'm sorry inspector, but I've already stated that there is no need for me to see the children after they've gone upstairs."

"Well sir, they say you did."

Freddie started to feel agitated because being told he was a liar, which is what the two police officers were implying, was beginning to unnerve him.

"Then they are mistaken and I'm afraid to say, not telling the truth."

"You own a Dell laptop?" queried Sergeant Philips.

"Yes I do, it's very old and not very reliable."

"But do you watch pornography on it?" Inspector Brown lobbed his question in like a hand grenade

Freddie went pink and said "I think you ought to leave as your personal questions about my life are out of order."

"That may well be your opinion sir, but let me tell you where we are coming from. Tania Vlassa has given a statement asserting that after she was ordered upstairs to bed by you, some fifteen minutes later when she was in her nightdress and reading a book for the following days exams, you entered her bedroom, sat on her bed and started fondling her chest. She claims that you then unzipped your trousers, pulled out your penis and started fingering her vagina. You grabbed her head and forced it to touch your member. At this time she was screaming and struggling. At which point she says that her brother, disturbed by the noise, came into the bedroom. Toby Vlassa's testimony confirms this and adds that when he approached the bed you yanked his pyjama trousers down and pulled his penis out saying 'I expect you want some of this as well'. They both say that they are making such a noise and struggling that you get up, pull up your trousers and leave saying you are sorry, and they shouldn't say anything to their parents as they won't be believed if they did."

Freddie is gasping, open mouthed like a fish out of water.

"But this is preposterous, it's a complete fabrication. I know the kids dislike, even hate me, but this is simply incredible."

"Well sir, we need a formal statement from you and need you to accompany us to Camden police station for a recorded interview. We will also, if you have no objection, take the Dell pc with us. Otherwise we will obtain a court order to seize it."

Dazed and bewildered, Freddie stands up, his knees almost buckling as he attempts to walk to the door with the restraining hand of Detective Inspector Ian Brown on his shoulder.

Freddie subconsciously already suspects that calamitous forces are gathering around him. The train is hurtling into a darkening tunnel and no-one but no-one will extend a helping hand.

Almost fearfully he asks as he leaves his little world behind him, whether he will be allowed to return.

"Not for me to say sir" replies the inspector but softens the reply by saying that in cases like this the accused is usually free on bail until the court hearing.

Even as he speaks, Ian Brown's years of experience with all types of crime and criminals sends him a tiny flutter of apprehension that this poor, inoffensive, little man may be heading for an undeserved guillotine.

Sitting in the back of the police car, Freddie, shaking and sweating with almost catatonic panic, whispers "But I don't have any money for bail. I have no family and all my friends, if they exist after this, are all part time actors and are as skint as I am."

Again the Inspector replies: "Not for me to say sir, it's up to the Magistrates to determine whether there is a case to answer, whether bail is necessary."

Staring mutely at the tiled walls of his holding cell, Freddie desperately tries to hold his world together. He is offered tea but spills most of it as his hands are shaking so much as if he has contracted Parkinson's Disease. After what seems like eternity but in reality only half hour, he is led into the interview room.

Gloomy and impersonal, conveying a subtle psychological message of implied guilt: "Look mate, we all know what you've done, cop for it and we can all go home early."

Freddie is introduced to the duty solicitor, whose damp handshake, greasy hair, thin lips and patch of stubble under his nose where the early morning razor missed its mark, illustrates the fact that not all solicitors are earning 'city' salaries and bonuses. He asks for a few moments privately with his client and immediately crushes Freddie's hope of early justice by saying that if Freddie confesses to a charge of minor assault there could be a lesser prison sentence, even the possibility of a suspended sentence and a hefty fine.

Freddie's last shred of self-respect throws itself into the ring, and without looking the lawyer in the eye says in a quaking voice: "I have no money, I am innocent of whatever they are trying to throw at me. If you are not prepared to defend me then I will stand up for myself on my own."

Graham Mercer, the duty solicitor merely shrugs and says "You cannot be really stupid enough to do that, so let's see what they have to throw at you."

There is no contest. Freddie is confronted with the sworn statements of the Vlassa twins, and, despite his protestations that he is being set up, the duty solicitor simply agrees that Freddie is free to return home with a police constable and surrender his passport.

A glimmer of the old Freddie weakly attempts a flash of humour. "Passport? I've never had enough money to travel abroad, unless you count the Isle of Wight and don't even think of a driving license, the nearest I've ever been to a car is on the dodgems."

The flat is the same as when he left it. Or is it? Now it has a strange sense of menace. This may not be home much longer.

Chapter 4

Gregory Vlassa knots his tie and says to Trisha Ellson hurriedly pulling her panties up: "Now that's what sex is all about, not some creepy pervert diddling young children."

Trisha nods knowing that Vlassa has a passion about his crusade to rid the world of homosexual, perverts and socialists, though not necessarily in that order. Strangely, marital infidelity and his dubious sex demands do not loom large on his radar screen.

An hour later Gregory Vlassa is enjoying a refreshing gin and tonic at his club. Across the bar, he spies Quentin Cameron, a recently appointed crown court judge. Through his newspaper contacts, Vlassa has gleaned that Cameron is a closet bigot. Gregor, his poisonous Aide de Camp has also discovered that Cameron himself was abused as a child at home and bullied at school. His small stature brought further humiliation as his classmates dubbed him with the pseudonym 'silly willy'. Determined to get his own back, law seemed as good as any route to achieve social standing and even maybe lock up some of his school day detractors.

Gregory Vlassa needed no further ammunition to enlist Quentin Cameron on his mission to rid the world of child abusers and sex offenders.

"Join me in a gin and tonic old boy." Vlassa knew that Cameron could not resist the opportunity to suck up to his ideologue. Fawning like a lovesick lap dog, Vlassa was always amused to think that one day, wringing his hands, Cameron would repeat those immortal words from Charles Dickens' Scrooge "Ever so humble, sir."

"Understand you're trying the Wharburton case, Quentin?" Cameron blinked, not sure how this information could have travelled so fast, but then, newspaper moguls have their own sources.

"Well yes, not sure how public the news is."

"Don't worry; I won't be publishing anything until the appointment is confirmed. But," Vlassa continued, "I am sure that you are sensitive enough to realise that a salutary sentence will send the right message to these evil bastards, and won't do your prospects of a high court appointment any harm at all. Not to say the least it will earn the very favourable support of my media channels."

Quentin Cameron puffed himself up and after taking a long slurp of his drink said: "Have no doubts on that score Gregory, if I may call you that. I will see justice is seen to be done and no mistake."

You sycophantic little shit, thought Vlassa, but playing to the gallery replied: "Thought I could rely on you, let's have another G&T, my shout."

Chapter 5

Freddie Wharburton arrived at Camden Crown Court having no idea that he was already being served up to the guillotine, hanged, drawn and quartered by forces beyond his imagining.

There had been little attempt by his barrister to question the prospective jurors or query their backgrounds to unearth underlying prejudices. The lengths that the lawyers in Grisham's book 'the Runaway Jury' went to obtain a sympathetic panel had no resonance from Caradog Bartholomew. The briefing he had received from Freddie's solicitor clearly indicated that he was bang to rights and expensive time in his defence was pretty pointless.

The court was less than full as Freddie listened to the case outlined against him. The children's evidence was heard in camera and by video link where they were not actually seen, only heard by the jurors.

The evidence piled up against Freddie was relentless. The adult porn recorded on his computer; although the prosecuting QC did have the grace to concede that there was no evidence of child images; added more damaging characterisation of a sixty year old bachelor, never married, gaining qualifications so he could work with children.

Finally the prosecution turned to the judge and said that there was one recent piece of evidence supplied by the children that could prove crucial. Unfortunately there had been no time to offer it to the defence, so said QC Roger Lawrence.

"Could I ask your Honours indulgence and introduce it at this late stage?"

Justice Quentin Cameron, wanting to appear even handed said: "I will hear it on the understanding that if I think it will lead to a mistrial, I will stop you immediately."

"Believe me your Honour; I would not insult your impartiality if I did not think for one moment that this new evidence is vital."

"Very well, continue."

Freddie was recalled to the witness box and reminded that he was still under oath. His QC had briefly muttered to Freddie that this was highly unusual and did he have any clue to where this was going. By now Freddie had ceased to even think coherently. Nothing in his life had prepared him for this dissection of his whole being.
He barely heard the question being repeated.

"Mr Wharburton, could you please tell the court whether you have a brown mole or blemish on your penis."

Freddie looked in vain at his barrister who was busily looking through papers in front of him, ensuring that he would have no eye contact with his client.

"Do you understand the question Mr Wharburton?" pressed Roger Lawrence.

"Yes, yes" stammered Freddie.

"Is that a yes to whether you understand the question or a yes as to whether you have such a mark on your penis?"

Freddie looked at the judge and asked whether it was necessary to reply.

"You can have a break to ask your barrister but as I have already allowed the question, I'm sure you will be advised to answer it."

Freddie, already sensing that he was a beaten man, whispered in a hoarse voice.

"Well, there is a birth mark on my penis."

"Is it clearly visible to the naked eye?" Roger Lawrence on a roll was obviously prepared to ask Freddie to display his manhood in the witness box if necessary.

The judge realising this was an earth moving breakthrough weighed in.

"Come now Mr Wharburton, answer the question or I shall have you examined by the court doctor."

"Well, yes I suppose it is pretty visible."

Roger Lawrence returned to his desk and drew out two documents.

"These, your Honour are two transcripts and two recorded interviews held yesterday with the children, the innocent victims in this case. I will offer them as Exhibit A and B and whilst the learned defence counsel may ask for a recess to consider his clients response, I think that it will save much time if I read them now."

"Do you have any objections to your learned friends request?"

Caradog Bartholomew stood slowly and without glancing at his client said stonily, "I have no objection your honour, but reserve the right to ask for an adjournment to speak with my client after hearing what this is all about."

"Very well. Mr Lawrence, enter your evidence."

In slow measured tones Roger Lawrence read the first transcript made by the girl.

"When this man took out his thing and started to play with it, as it got longer I noticed this brown spot getting bigger. I am sorry I didn't mention it before but everything has been so awful I completely forgot."

Soft gasps could be heard around the court as the judge ordered the court usher to demand silence while the second transcript was read.

"When I came into Tania's bedroom and saw this man attempting to push his thing into my sister's mouth, I started to hit him but he pulled my pyjamas down as I said before. As my sister said, this mark was clearly visible on his penis. I did not think to mention this before and I am very sorry in case it is important."

"Your honour, I don't think that the prosecution has any more evidence to offer."

"Your witness, Mr Bartholomew."

Caradog Bartholomew hitched his gown over his shoulders as he stepped out from behind his desk.

"I have no further questions for my client, your honour."

Summing up, the prosecution barrister turned to the jury and simply said: "You have heard the evidence. There can be no reasonable doubt that Mr Wharburton misplaced the trust that was put in him by two loving parents and abused these two children. This man must be taken off the streets for a very long time to protect youngsters like these."

The defending barrister walked to the front of the jury box, clutching a pencil between his fingers as if it was his client's neck.

"You have heard the evidence. If you are minded to find my client guilty, I would ask you to remember that there is no previous history that he has ever been accused of behaviour like this. You may wish to believe his statements that this whole story is a plot by two very devious children who have long harboured a vendetta against him. If you have any doubt about who is telling the truth, you must return a not guilty verdict."

Judge Quentin Cameron in his summing up reiterated the last sentence of the defending barrister: "You are here to decide who is telling the truth." He concluded: "Consider the evidence, consider the personalities involved, consider who has to gain by making up such a lurid story and finally consider there are no lies when confronted with physical evidence that couldn't possibly be invented. Consider your verdict."

Freddie realised with prescient certainty that the judges final observation was his nemesis. Without actually saying it, the judge was tacitly directing the jury to use the blemish as the conclusive evidence of guilt.

Less than one hour later Freddie's worst nightmare became reality. The foreman of the jury when asked how do you find the defendant, guilty or not guilty, simply replied: "we find the defendant guilty as charged." When asked was this a majority verdict, he said this was the verdict of all twelve jurors.

Justice Quentin Cameron faced the courtroom and using his best sonorous tone said: "I firstly would like to thank the jury for their patience and studied calm attention during this distressing case. Their unanimous verdict reflects the realisation that the court was gradually unravelling a story of horrid perversion pursued by the defendant. It is my duty to send a message to anyone involved in such activity that they will be exposed and punished by the full weight of the law. Therefore it is my duty to sentence Frederick Wharburton to a term in prison of fifteen years with a recommendation that this is not subject to parole or early release."

As the guards moved to escort Freddie from the court, he almost collapsed in their arms. Two fat tears rolled down his cheeks as he whispered to no-one in particular, a last cry from within – "But I didn't do anything."

Many months later, Freddie lying awake in his cell, like Paul on the road to Damascus, had the vision that revealed how the children had learnt about the birth mark on his penis.

The house in NW8 is only a stone's throw from Regents Park Zoo. It was the only time the Vlassa's had asked Freddie to accompany the children on an expedition outside. That Saturday the Vlassa's were attending an important business colleague's party and asked Freddie to take the children to the zoo. During the afternoon Freddie and Toby visited the WC together. Standing alongside each other peeing into the trough, Toby, so much shorter, would have no problem glancing at Freddie's penis and observing the mark. Priming his sister to give confirmatory evidence would be as easy as telling all the lies they had colluded together.

Too late, even if anyone believed him, the system would not retry a unanimously agreed verdict. Freddie was banged up for fifteen long isolated years. Great train robbers are feted, paedophiles are reviled and shunned.

"Everyone in here is innocent," said the prison governor, "don't waste your time even thinking about looking for sympathy. If you want to leave here in one piece concentrate only on survival."

No one would visit Freddie or send him birthday or Christmas cards. The other cons in Wandsworth Prison, after the usual demeaning initiation insults and physical jostling, chose to ignore the pathetic little man who asked for nothing more than to be left alone in his misery.

Chapter 6

"Nailed the bastard," gloated Gregory Vlassa. "But we need much more decisive action from the police, government, the media and social agencies to eradicate these misfits from society."

Striding up and down his palatial office, Vlassa was expanding his vision of a purge that would not have been out of keeping in Nazi Germany.

"We are too soft, too politically correct, too reactive, not proactive in dealing with the threat that these scum represent. As a newspaper, I expect more dynamic and dramatic feature stories exposing the extent of the problem and how lenient we have become in tackling it."

The editorial staff of the Telegraph grunted in agreement. Yet another harangue from their owner, overturning all the promises of editorial independence when he bought the paper.

"But I am going to take my battle forward to a new level"

There was barely a sound as he dramatically raised his arms in the air.

"As a media owner my responsibility to the public needs a new forum, therefore I intend to enter parliament as an MP and fight our battle from within the influence of government."

He stopped and waited for a response from his troops. A smattering of applause gathered pace and soon all his staff were on their feet, voices raised, none wishing to be seen left out of the congratulatory buzz.

"Bravo sir, you'll do it!"

"Just what the country needs!"

"Open the champagne Trisha, my dear, and let's drink to victory."

Later down the local pub the self-same staff were reeling from their boss's pronouncement that they were all part of his mission to save the country.

"Jesus Fucking Christ," swore the business editor, "If I didn't have a wife, two kids and a mortgage to die for I would be out of this mad house faster than I can throw up."

"Who does he really think he is," queried the fashion editor, "a latter day Alfred Molseley?"

"Well," said another, "I agree with Charles (the business editor), I need my job and would remind you all not to state your opinions in front of Trisha Ellson. She not only has our dear proprietor's ear, but his fly buttons as well."

Left alone in the board room with her boss, Trisha Ellson knew that all this passion would soon translate into raw unbridled sex. As much as she resolved to resist and make her excuse to leave, the familiar wetness in her vagina breached her defences. Even so she was unprepared for the savagery of his sexual onslaught. Defiled, debased, Trisha sat naked on the floor in an orgasmic trance as they slurped champagne and sprayed it over each other.

A hour later after showering in his en-suite office flat, dressed as if nothing had happened, Trisha poured coffee from the Tassimo machine.

"So my dear leader, with three years of the present parliament to go, how do you plan to enter parliament as an MP?"

"MP! MP!? I'm not planning anything as short term as MP. My goal is Prime Minister, nothing less will serve me, my causes and the country!"

Trisha stared at her boss and for the first time since becoming involved with him wondered whether he was sane or suffering from the same delusion of grandeur that put people in mental asylums.

"OK, sorry to be so unimaginative, but practically how can you enter parliament without first standing for a seat?"

"That my dear is for you to find out. From Monday your sole task is to unearth a constituency with an incumbent conservative MP who may be conducive or, and I say this reluctantly, coerced into a change of career direction."

"You mean bribe him or her to go?"

"Whatever it takes my dear. Now get on home for a good weekends rest. You have a busy week ahead of you."

Monday morning, a freshly reinvigorated personal assistant started the laborious task of analysing every conservative constituency MP in the country. Actually its not that difficult. Despite what the media tries to imply, most MPs have fairly stable, even ordinary lives with wives, families, mortgages, HP debt, the same as their beloved voters. But a few have quirks and kinks in their personal lives that can always risk being exploited or exposed.

It was only Wednesday when Trisha sought a meeting with Gregory Vlassa

"I think I've found your seat" she exclaimed triumphantly.

"His name is Bernard Mayhew MP for a remote Cambridge constituency. After his wife died 20 years ago, he never remarried. Children long gone to live in Canada and Australia. He is well regarded as a local MP but rarely raises his head above the parapet in parliament. Aged 58, he is perceived as slightly aloof by the locals. But who, despite his sort of personal remoteness, has never been challenged for the seat over the past four general elections."

Gregory Vlassa licked his lips and sighed.

"I like him already. I think we should send one of our reporters to interview him as a sort of pilot for an in depth character series. 'Do you really know your MP?'" Trisha rose and said: "I'll get my secretary to arrange an appointment."

"No, not you my treasure, ask Gregor to come in, there are a few matters I wish to raise with him."

"Well, why not me? I found him for you and I am supposed to be a journalist!"

Trisha's indignation cut no ice as Gregory dismissed her anger by saying:

"This is far too junior for you, wait till the story develops then I'll hand it over."

Mystified at this vague hint of more to come, Trisha had no option but to leave and ushered Gregor into the office.

Chapter 7

She was 22 years of age, flawless skin, blue eyes, blonde shoulder length hair, legs up to her armpits and a smile that would put a blowtorch to shame. Dressed in a white silk blouse with a décolletage that promised 36D cup breasts to die for and a black skirt that echoed the essayists dictum, 'long enough to cover the point but short enough to be interesting', Cindy was the dream journalist every MP craves to be interviewed by.

The short journey from Cambridge railway station to his office had already forced Bernard Mayhew MP to refocus on his driving several times. The thighs next to him as the skirt gently slid upwards became the most intoxicating purveyors of flesh he had seen in years. It was hard to concentrate on the questions this vision of sensational beauty was putting to him. Almost like a school boy on his first date, Bernard Mayhew spluttered his responses, pinkly embarrassed by his all too obvious fascination with Cindy's cleavage. When she finally suggested after snuggling her notebook into her Gucci handbag that her employer the ever generous Daily Record, a sleazy tabloid few knew Vlassa owned, would be pleased to offer Mr Mayhew lunch did he realise that he had died and gone to heaven. Cindy had obviously done her homework as they retired to an old country inn on the outskirts of the city that even on his salary and expenses Bernard had never had the nerve to visit.

Conversation died in the dining room as this ill matched couple walked in. He didn't care and it made him feel like a million dollars. An afternoon and lifetime away, they walked along the bank of the river. Cindy, hanging on to his every word, and Bernard trying desperately to hang on to his sanity.

They stopped in a riverside pub and Bernard was aware of the pressure of the girls thighs against his as they drank beer in the snug bar. Not used to alcohol in general, an afternoon with the intoxicating Cindy had inflated Bernard's ego to unheard of heights. He almost swooned when she accepted his offer for dinner and perhaps, she coyly suggested, a night cap at his house before she REALLY had to return to her hotel.

Trisha Ellson was abruptly summoned from home to Gregory Vlassa's office at 6am the following morning.

"Get down to Cambridge Police HQ immediately! A local MP has been accused of the attempted rape of a young journalist. It could be sensational and yet another example of corrupt and venal politicians thinking they can do what they like and get away with it."

"Is she one of ours?" Trisha was trying hard to remember a vague conversation with her boss about a series featuring politicians.

"Certainly not" lied Vlassa.

"Well how did we get onto this story so soon? There's nothing on the news wires this morning even hinting about such a scandal."

"For fuck sake do what you're paid to do and get down there and cover the story!"

Knowing that further argument was pointless, Trisha grabbed her notebook and drove recklessly to Cambridge. This stinks she thought as she stormed down the M11. How can he know before anyone else? Unless...

The unbidden thought popped itself into mind as she grimly realised that once again her Svengali had somehow made the puppets dance to his tune.

The desk officer led Trisha to a comfortable waiting room, offered a coffee and left her to imagine how Gregory could have known.

The investigating officer Det. Inspector Frank Middleton shook hands and said; "I'll be as brief as I can. At 2am this morning a young girl by the name of Cindy Richardson came into the station in a highly distressed state. Her clothes were dishevelled, blouse torn and scratches on her face. She claimed that having accepted the offer of a night cap by our local MP Bernard Mayhew, after interviewing him during the day and over dinner, he started to make improper advances which she resisted. Finally he tried to assault her physically but she fought him off. Probably because he had been drinking on and off all day, he fell, hit his head and went down on the floor. Realising that she had to do something that she called the local police. We immediately sent a car and ambulance to his house to find him fast asleep on the sofa (where she said she had put him). After being checked by the paramedics, we woke him and brought him here, where, after he came round earlier this morning, cautioned him and later charged him for sexual assault and attempted rape."

"But by her admission he was as drunk as a skunk", Trisha observed.

"That's not for me to judge", said Inspector Middleton. Date rape is no excuse by law and in my experience the higher you are the harder you fall."

Hardly had he spoken than Trisha Ellson's mobile rang.

"Are you ready to file the story yet?" barked a subby in the editorial department. "We can use it for a mid-morning slot on our TV news and radio channels."

Dully, Trisha repeated the story from the inspector verbatim. Strangely, Cindy Richardson had disappeared, no one quite knew when she left the station and no one seemed to have an accurate home address or telephone number.

Notwithstanding, the following mornings headline in the Telegraph screamed:

'LOCAL MP ACCUSED OF RAPE BY 22 YEAR OLD JOURNALIST.'

Extraordinary, that despite her strange presence by her absence, a clear photograph of a beautiful, innocent young girl was pictured side by side in the article with one of a very haggard distraught looking MP from rural Cambridgeshire.

Without knocking, Trisha Ellson flung herself into Vlassa's office.

"You bastard, you absolute bastard. You set the poor bastard up. I've a good mind to reveal what I know and give this poor sod the break he deserves."

"My dear, my dear, calm yourself."

Gregory Vlassa's liquid voice embraced her as he firmly pushed her into one of the overstuffed office armchairs.

"I don't know what you are so upset about. Whoever the young lady was, and she wasn't one of ours, no one deserves to be attacked by a middle age pervert"

"I bet Gregor knows who she is."

Gregory's voice turned to ice. "Never make accusations to me that you cannot prove. I can break you with a snap of my fingers. You owe everything you have to me. Do not ever think of threatening me again do you hear me? When you joined up for the ride there was no option to get off the roller coaster when you started to feel queasy. You fuck with me and I'll fuck you as I've always done, with or without your approval!"

Silently, Trisha left his office before he could unzip his pants. Returning to her car in the underground car park she wept as she had never done before for the age of innocence that she knew she had left for ever.

Two days later the media reported that the local MP accused of rape had committed suicide in his home by hanging himself from a rafter in his garage. Trisha read the note he left behind in which he claimed that the false accusations were making his life unbearable and his constituents did not deserve to be represented by someone who would always live under the shadow, whether proven or not, of being a rapist. "I can only apologise to my family, my friends and supporters."

Accessory to suicide is not a recognised crime but, thought Trisha, if it was I'd be in the front row.

Chapter 8

"Well", commented Vlassa blithely, "What a turn up for the books. A perfect constituency for my place in parliament, and whilst one feels sorry for Mr Mayhew, family and friends, life has a way of opening one door as another closes.

Alexandria Vlassa looked at her husband with undisguised contempt.

"What a load of sanctimonious humbug Gregory. You cannot wait to dance on his grave. I don't know what part you played, if any, in his convenient demise and I don't want to know but don't play mind games with me, I know you too well."

"Then there's nothing more to be said."

Gregory looked flushed, like a boy caught with his fingers in the cookie jar. It wasn't often these days that he even came home, but to be pilloried by his wife added to a vague sense of unease that his part in Mayhew's death was overstepping the mark of civilised behaviour even by his debased standards.

Pacing up and down his penthouse office suite, Vlassa had soon forgotten his wife's remarks and ordered his secretary to contact the chairman of the rural Cambridge constituency and make an appointment as soon as conveniently possible.

"Before you ring him, scout round for the best restaurant locally and invite him to join me for lunch, I bet he'll wet his knickers. These jumped up local politicians are all the same, one finger stuffed up their arse, the other jammed in the till."

His secretary flushed but, as usual, kept her thoughts and retorts to herself.

Major Alfred Withington (retired) was almost bursting with pride and bonhomie as he met Vlassa at the local village railway station. A nice touch arriving by train thought Vlassa. Man of the people, energy saving, not polluting the rural environment with the merest whiff of fumes from his Bentley.

"My dear chap, honoured to meet you. Hope the journey was not too exhausting. Do you need the facilities? Let's go to my constituency office where we can enjoy tea or would you prefer coffee and some of my wife's cakes, baked specially for the occasion. Not too many mark you, don't want to spoil lunch do we?"

As they drove in his freshly polished 8 year old Renault Megane, Withington could hardly pause for breath as he nervously tried to put his guest at ease.

To Vlassa, who was aware of the effect his presence had on people like Withington, the noise simply went over his head. Once in Withington's office however, Gregory Vlassa used his personal authority to dominate the meeting.

"Frankly Alfred, I am devastated that you should have lost such a devoted local MP in these tragic circumstances. But I will not beat about the bush with you as I can see you're a man who will not have the wool pulled over his eyes."

Alfred Withington was almost purring from these compliments poured upon him. Definitely a man after his own heart, too damned right!

"Let me come directly to the point."

Vlassa stood up and almost saw the Major sink into his chair as he moved to the front of his desk.

"I imagine that you have many local, fine upstanding candidates to be considered for this seat. But to put it bluntly, none of them can bring to the party what I have to offer if you select me as your parliamentary candidate. My media channels, me, a well-known personality with clearly stated views about the future of our society and a substantial cash budget available to be fed into the system. Take one example, you are constituency chairman with many meetings to attend around the county and other political committees further afield. Your 8 year old car frankly, in my view, is not its best age for the job. I am sure that on your pension a new car is not the highest priority but I have a pool of brand new company cars one of which could easily be donated to you."

Major Withington did not know whether he was being justifiably rewarded for his years of service to the cause or simply bribed. But, over lunch at the two star restaurant, out of bounds to he and wife, he persuaded himself that Vlassa was simply recognising the truth that a very industrious constituency chairman could not be let down by an unreliable car, and yes, if Vlassa did get the job, a new BMW 325i would certainly fit the bill.

What Vlassa didn't know, and what Withington was not going to enlighten him, was that the constituency was facing a crisis. Membership had fallen, reserves to fight an election were perilously low, but more alarming was the fact that the Lib Dem candidate was a very popular local figure.

Senior partner in a very well established solicitors practice with several branches around the constituency, David Burke was well known and well respected. His work on the council was always well reported and it was likely that the efforts on his local ward garnered him votes from Conservatives as well as his own Lib Dems.

Major Alfred Withington did not want a seat at the next general election to be lost on his watch. Sod the locals! Bring on the big guns!

"Don't worry about me Alfred, I'll get a taxi to the station, don't want you unable to drive your new car".

Alfred's look of alarm set Vlassa off soothing him.

"Only joking old boy, I know you will set the ball rolling to choose the most suitable candidate, and certainly I won't presume to foresee the outcome."
Withington visibly relaxed as Vlassa left the restaurant. Getting into the taxi, Vlassa warmly shook his hand, and holding it as politicians do, said:

"Whatever happens I have enjoyed my day here and learning about the issues that concern the local folk, issues you can be sure would be a focus of my manifesto. Personally it has been a privilege to spend time with you and my assurance that together we can maintain the Conservative heritage."

Flattered, bemused and overwhelmed, Withington surrendered to a final hug and returned to the restaurant bar to celebrate a gift from heaven. He would ensure that the selection committee would see things his way and even if the BMW was slightly questionable, it was after all, only a car!

Chapter 9

It was an electoral contest but then it was never a real contest. Vlassa's publicity machinery moved into top gear and he moved into a local rented apartment right in the heart of the constituency. This was no arm's length candidate. Every day and many evenings Gregory Vlassa went out pressing the flesh, visiting schools, hospitals, police stations and old people's homes.

David Burke did his best but attempting to canvas whilst running a busy daytime practice meant it could never be a level playing field.

Apart from which, playing to the gallery was Vlassa's forte, and an innocent public fell for his physical dynamism and often charismatic public speaking.

The returning officer was able to declare Gregory Vlassa elected as a Member of Parliament for the constituency after one of the quickest vote counts in years. His majority trumped Burke by a massive 35% returning him to parliament with one of the largest ever seen in recent history.

"Now the work really starts," grunted Vlassa after a particularly energetic sexual bout with Trisha Ellson.

"No more beating around the bush, let's get these bastards on the run."

Trisha opened a bottle of Dom Perignon and thought they haven't got a clue what they've let themselves in for, but it ain't gonna take long to find out.

Thoughts echoed by the Prime Minister, Michael Allders, who initially had welcomed Gregory Vlassa into parliament with open arms.

"A fresh insight into the business of running the country," intoned Allders at a small reception at number 10. "We don't often get successful businessmen, still running multi-million pound corporations, entering parliament. They usually wait till they're retired and tout for a seat in the Lords."

"Well Prime Minister" responded Vlassa raising his glass of House of Commons house white wine.

"I've never been one for convention and I believe my current ongoing business experience could be put to good use at a senior level in your government."

Vlassa had to restrain himself from stating the obvious – "in your cabinet."

"Quite so." responded Allders, who was only too aware of the implication. I'm sure it won't take too long for me to find something useful for you to do."

Vlassa gritted his teeth, always one to speak his mind, and with enough money to sometimes pay off an irritating obstacle, knew that the subtle social game of nice nice had to be played.

He was kept waiting for ten days fuming and fretting. Not even regular sex with his assistant alleviated his impatience. Finally the call came. A long expected cabinet reshuffle meant that Allders could justifiably invite Vlassa to take up the position of Business Minister.

The expression 'better the enemy inside the camp looking out than outside the camp looking in' was about to be turned on its head. Michael Allders from day one realised that he had invited the viper into the nest.

Chipping away at his authority, Allders all too soon realised that nothing would satisfy Gregory Vlassa more than his job. It soon became clear that Vlassa was using his cabinet position to promote his political agenda way beyond his business department remit. It was not difficult for him to maximise his media exposure simply because he owned much of it.

"I don't know how much more of this I can take."

Michael Allders, clearly stressed, turned to his wife in the Number 10 flat.

"His constant sniping is ambushing me at every cabinet meeting. Worse, he has established a popular public rapport with his virtually neo fascist policies. Half the cabinet, I am sorry to say, would probably support him if it came to open revolt."

"Well my love, you've never been one to duck a political fight, but I hate to see you exhausted like this. However, if you do surrender now the country will face a future led by a closet, unbalanced demagogue. But if push comes to shove and you are ousted, it will more than suit me for us to retire to our cottage in Devon and watch the scene unravel without being near the civil unrest that he might provoke."

"I'll give it my best shot," replied Allders, "but don't hold your breathe. This bastard has more tentacles than Captain Nemo's octopus and just as deadly."

Two weeks later the country waited with bated breath as the long expected cabinet showdown gathered pace.

Vlassa had conjured together a cabal of cabinet ministers who wanted decisive action on restoring the death penalty, certainly for police murder (but why stop there?!), renegotiating the terms of Common Market membership, re-opening the debate about bringing back grammar schools, swingeing restrictions on every type of immigrant, legal and illegal, compulsory possession of national identity cards and no parole sentences for child abusers and paedophiles. A policy hotch-potch in short, beyond every 'Daily Mail' readers wildest dreams.

For the Metropolitan Police, the possibility of a return of the Thatcher era meant dusting down riot training manuals. The Commissioner was old enough to remember the cavalry charges across the Yorkshire Moors with a heightened sense of foreboding that it should happen again.

Chapter 10

"He's going down!" exclaimed Vlassa to Trisha back in his office. "Another day or two and the country will be in my hands."

Trisha Ellson realised that Vlassa had finally put into words his stark ambition to emasculate the British constitution.

Chapter 11

Framlingham Hall, public school for boys, nestles in the Suffolk countryside. It is a lesser known school than Eton or Harrow but its traditions reach back just as far.

Vlassa had chosen the school for his son, Toby, because of its fine history of producing resounding sportsmen, refined scholars and respected public servants. His son, was as a result of Vlassa's financial munificence to the schools funds, given excessive leeway for his not infrequent ill-considered behaviour towards his fellow school mates and his equally long suffering teachers. In short, Toby Vlassa was a domineering, self-centred loathsome thug. But no one could ignore the unwelcome truth, that Toby Vlassa was a prodigy. He excelled at every subject and physical task that was thrown at him. Even more galling to his detractors was that he was handsome to the point of beautiful. The dark eastern looks inherited from his father together with the lithesome figure of his mother had yielded an offspring that gave no hint to the devil horns sprouting from his forehead. Stories of his cruelty to man and beast were legendary, and even if some were apocryphal, they in no way dented Vlassa's apocalyptic vision of himself.

One year younger, Justin Collingham at fifteen was almost the opposite of the school swimming champion he challenged. Blue eyed, blonde hair, a gentle and caring nature he was as far removed from Vlassa's glowering, bombastic and bullying character as chalk and cheese.

However, Justin was deeply in love. Shame it wasn't the school matron or the visiting French locum teacher. A fumbling encounter with Toby Vlassa in the schools swimming pool changing rooms signalled a new direction that would change his life.

Theirs became a super-heated relationship that left them both breathless with its unexpected intensity. Concealing their passionate physical bonding required ingenuity that only money can buy. But not even love and sexual congress could entirely overwhelm the truth.

As much as Justin was sublimely devoted to Toby Vlassa, there was a corner of his heart and mind that knew his paramour was inherently evil.

It was in post coital languor that the two lovers began desultorily talking in hushed tones about their lives. Toby Vlassa was the first to open up the conversation into the elicit excitement of their gay relationship.

"So my beautiful lover what is the most excessive and darkest secret you have hidden in your fifteen year old life?".

Justin shifted uncomfortably and wished the interrogation would move in another, less invasive direction. But as ever the imperative seduction in Toby's voice overcame his reticence to open his soul.

"I suppose Toby, my deepest fear is to be exposed as a homosexual to my parents, family and childhood friends. I come from a background that cannot really contemplate sexual aberration."

Whatever the failings of Framlingham Hall, teaching a comprehensive command of the English language was not one of them.

"Are you really that embarrassed?" scoffed Toby Vlassa.

"Well you asked me my secret, so that's it. I don't suppose you have anything like that Toby, you are so upfront about everything, being regarded as a queer probably doesn't faze you at all."

Toby glared at his companion and spat "Don't you ever use the word queer to describe us. We are not perverted like some old fart I know. My sister and I sealed his fate years ago and good riddance to him."

Intrigued, Justin tentatively said, "Go on Toby, you can't stop now what happened?"

Aware that for years he had wanted an audience to share his awesome story with, Toby, in his poshest public school voice gloatingly recounted the trial and conviction of Freddie Wharburton.

"Isn't it simply delicious," chortled Toby.

"So you mean that he wasn't guilty at all, you and your sister made it all up? Wow Toby, you really are something else."

Uncertain as to whether Justin was praising him or reappraising him, Toby shifted on the bed. Peering at his naked friend he started to experience a familiar urge and soon both were feasting on each other's bodies.

Justin's misgivings about his friend's revelations were temporarily submerged by a flood of sex swamping his senses.

Chapter 12

Cranham House sits regally overlooking Sherbourne village green. It is a fitting home for one of Her Majesty's senior civil servants. Dressed in yellow corduroys, Tattenham check shirt, dark brown brogue shoes and enveloped in a cloud of pipe tobacco smoke, Charles Collingham looked every inch the part.

He looked up from his Daily Telegraph to acknowledge his son stepping nervously into his study. Charles has never quite got used to being a father so he waits patiently for Justin to say something.

"Dad," and then a pause, "Have you got a minute?"

Charles waved his son to a leather armchair by the fire, and moving from his desk, sits in the chair opposite.

"Sure son, what's on your mind?"

"Dad, look, I don't know how to explain this and I really think I do know what it means, but you tell me, what is perjury?"

The civil servant in Charles rises to the occasion.

"It is the telling of a deliberate lie under oath in a court of law either by the defendant or the prosecution does not matter."

Not sure what has provoked the question, but concerned by his sons obvious discomfiture, Charles offers to get down his Oxford English dictionary to confirm his definition.

"No, no dad, I'm sure you're right."

"So is this something to do with a school project?" Charles asked.

"There are plenty of examples of quite famous people who have been caught out perjuring themselves in court. An easy example is Jeffrey Archer and he was sentenced to 2 years in prison. It is regarded as a very serious offence which eats at the heart of justice if left unpunished."

Charles is now quite perplexed as his son sits opposite him, pink faced and clenching and unclenching his hands. As often in the past he wonders how he and his wife gave birth to such a beautiful son.

Another pause, and then Justin blurted out "Dad I'm gay. I'm sorry but you have to know."

Charles sat back and re-lit his pipe. Gazing quite calmly at his son, said after a moment: "Your mother and I have sometimes wondered but never wondered enough to ask."

Justin stared over his father's shoulder and asked simply,

"Why not? I'm your son, doesn't every parent want to know?"

Charles knew this was a defining moment in their relationship and desperately hoped he wasn't about to blow it when he replied:

"Justin, you are our son, we love you without conditions. We brought you into the world and for as long as you want us in yours, we are one family. Anyway son, who knows..." Charles gave a faint smile and continued, "it may only be a passing teenage experiment, but whatever, you must never, ever doubt our love for you."

Justin pushed back in the armchair, and after catching his father's eye said "Dad, there's more. Jesus, Dad, this is so gross, but I can't let it rest. Now I know you and mum are looking out for me. I desperately need some help and advice.

Charles said "I'm listening."

In shaky, hesitant, stark sentences Justin recounted his affair with Toby Vlassa.

Somewhat startled by his sons lover's name, he queried, "you mean the son of Gregory Vlassa, the media mogul and frankly probably not the most popular star in the universe."

"Yes, him. And now to my shame his son is probably just as culpable of being a complete shit."

Justin with increasing confidence related the conversation with Toby Vlassa culminating in his obvious glee in seeing Freddie jailed for 15 years for something which he was patently innocent.

"Trouble is dad, I feel like an accessory to a crime, that although I am not responsible for, now I know I cannot simply sit back and let this poor man serve the rest of his sentence. But what can I do?"

"Well two things son, firstly, you have my over-whelming admiration for your courage in telling me about this appalling travesty of justice and secondly, being a senior civil servant does have its advantages. Do nothing more yourself. I have a route to some very high ranking police officers who can set wheels in motion with ultimate discretion. I cannot advise you how to handle your relationship with Toby when you return to school but it may be best to see if you can distance yourself gradually from him. If this turns out as I suspect it may, there could be some very unpleasant fallout. I could suggest that you don't return to school and we find you another one but I think this may send Toby Vlassa running for cover and spoil the chances of getting a fair hearing for Freddie."

"Dad you are a star! You will tell mum won't you?"

"Of course! She deserves to know what a magnificent son she has. Now let's go down for dinner and I think we should all enjoy a few well deserved glasses of wine tonight."

As Justin returned to school apprehensive about his friendship with Toby, but buoyed by his parents support, Charles returned to his office and immediately set wheels in motion to see if there are genuine grounds to re-open the case.

Chief Superintendent Adrian Simpson needed little encouragement to send a very dainty and feminine fast-track officer to the West Country. Like many other police officers, he resented many of the slurs, innuendos and downright insults the police endured at the hands of some of Vlassa's media mouthpieces. He had known Ian Brown as an Inspector shortly before he retired and respected his reputation for shrewdness and honestly.

"Sergeant Madelaine Coulsdon to see you, dear," called Janet Brown from the front door of their pretty Devon cottage in Aveton Gifford.

Wearing faded brown corduroy trousers and plaid shirt, Ian Brown couldn't have looked more retired if he'd tried. Over tea and cakes Madelaine explained the background to why she had called.

Putting well gardened hands on his knees, Ian Brown took some moments to reply.

"Do you know, my dear", he said, "although poor Freddie was banged to rights with the evidence of the twins, the evidence of the porn and ultimately the revelation of the mole or whatever on his penis, I never quite shook off the suspicion that here was a man never capable of doing what he was accused. If you feel that I could be of any help in re-interviewing the children I would be only too pleased to help. There was something eerily sanctimonious about them that by hindsight could have blindsided all of us!"

Round a conference table at New Scotland Yard, Madelaine Coulsdon voiced her opinion to Chief Superintendent Simpson and Assistant Commissioner Kenneth Robinson.

"We could be looking at a very distinct possibility that Mr Wharburton was stitched up, but getting the children to corroborate is another matter. At present we only have Justin's testimony, and if Toby Vlassa denies it we are stumped."

"Pulling rabbits out of a hat so to speak" said Simpson, "Could we get Justin to wear a tape and get Toby Vlassa to repeat the story to him? He obviously gets his rocks off on his personal notoriety."

Turning to his father, Charles Collingham, the Assistant Commissioner asked

"What do you think Charles; could we ask Justin to try it?"

"Well he's home for half term this coming weekend so it's as good a time as any. I think he feels so mortified by his friends' behaviour. Yes I'm sure he would give it a go. But if it is to be during another lovers tryst, and God I hate to be party to my sons involvement, you had better ensure the bug is well hidden if you get my drift."

"Don't worry Charles; it will be state of the art."

Chapter 13

Pacing up and down his sumptuous office, Vlassa gloated to Trisha

"I am nearly there; the whole cabinet is running around like chickens with their heads cut off. One final push and they will ditch the PM without so much as a bye or leave."

"Are you so certain he will go without a last rear guard action?"

"What can he do to stop me? From cancelling so called gay marriages to my euro-sceptic overtones, the country is behind me. He is isolated and bloody well knows it. But you're right, he's dead, but won't lie down, yet."

In the midst of this tirade they hardly noticed Gregor slipping into the office.

"Um boss, could I have a word, um I've just heard what you've said and, um, what I've heard could create some rather awkward problems."

"Well, go on man" boomed Vlassa, "We haven't got all day. Has the press got hold of some speeding conviction of mine from years ago, or what?"

"Um, it could be more serious than that."

"For Christ's sake spit it out, I've got a country to run"

Gregor took a deep breath and started,

"You know, sir, that you pay me to pay several informers in the Met police."

"Yes, yes I know, get on with it."

"Well one of them has got wind of a rather serious investigation about to be opened regarding Toby."

"So what's the little tyke been up to? Shagging sheep in the local Suffolk countryside?"

Gregory Vlassa winked at Trisha as he guffawed at his own humour.

Gregor shifted from foot to foot and almost cringed as he said "um, well actually not sheep, one of the other schoolboys."

"What are you saying you half-witted twat, that my sons been accused of being a queer, a faggot, a poof, GAY?"

"Um, well it's slightly more serious than that."

"Look I haven't got all day, what is it you are trying to tell me, and if you say 'um' once more I'll ram it down your throat."

Gregor looked at the floor as he muttered.

"The boy that he has been seeing has told the police that Toby and his sister made up the story seven years ago that put Freddie Wharburton in prison. Apparently Toby confessed to this during one of their err, um, sessions."

There was total silence. Just about every expression from rage to disgust flitted across Gregory Vlassa's face. At last he managed to control his breathing to grate: "You do realise if this becomes public I am ruined. My parliamentary career will be over and I'll be the laughing stock of the country."

He paused and said "Who, apart from this other faggot knows anything about this?"

"I'm not entirely sure," ventured Gregor, "But my informer leads me to believe they are waiting for Justin, the other lad, to obtain more evidence."

"Right," Gregory Vlassa, regaining his composure strode over the office floor to the wall safe concealed behind a painting behind his desk. Twirling the dials with a ferocity that almost made them overheat, Vlassa seized a bundle of notes.

"Here's £25.000, fix it and fix it good. I don't even want to think about this resurfacing. Do you hear me? Everything and everyone has a price, just pay it and make it go away, permanently."

Gregor went over to the waste bin beside the desk and lifted out the plastic liner. He stuffed the wads of cash into the bag and stared with his bovine eyes at his employer.

"Trust me boss, I'll fix it good."

Turning to leave, he glowered at Trisha who he both feared and desired at the same time. He knew the moment he left the office; his boss would be devouring her without thought to whether her devotion to Gregory matched his.

Chapter 14

It only took a brief knock at the door for it to be opened by Charles Collingham. Confronted by a middle age man and a younger petite pretty female, Charles first thoughts were to say, "Sorry we're not interested." Double glazing, Jehovah's witnesses, insurance salesmen all received the same polite but firm rejection.

But today, if only they were one of those.

Gently clearing his throat, the gent, who Charles absently thought looks like a policeman, said:

"I am sorry Sir, to intrude but are you Charles Collingham?"

"Well, yes I am, can I help you?"

"I am Chief Superintendent Adrian Simpson and this is DS Madelaine Coulsdon, could we come in as we have something to tell you. If your wife is home she may wish to be present."

Sensing that this was not a routine call to do with his job, Charles stepped aside and gestured for them to move into the lounge.

"What is it dear, who are these people?" Charles wife came in from the garden dressed as only middle class, Middle English wives do when pruning the roses.

"They are from the police."

"I can only say this with greatest sympathy, but your son was run down by a hit and run driver this afternoon as he was walking along the pavement near the gates to his school. The paramedics who attended the accident said he was killed instantly. Because this is the subject of a police inquiry, the school were asked not to contact you until we were able to inform you. I cannot say how sorry we are to bring this horrendous news, but I can say that we will do everything humanly possible to catch the person responsible."

The police officers looked on helplessly as the couple stood clutching each other wordlessly. They seemed like damaged balloons with the air slowly draining from them. The middle aged lines on their faces seemed to fracture even deeper as each second passed.

"But he was our only child, our only son, he cannot be gone like this!"

The silent tears flowed down both their faces. The nightmare that parents read about in the press about other families tragedies was now their own.

"Do you have any idea who, why or what happened?"

Charles tried to keep his voice level, as he attempted to bring some sense of reality into the bomb blast that had detonated into their lives.

DS Madelaine Coulsdon said in her soft west country accent:

"We know it was a dark green saloon, no one could read the number plate. It mounted the curb at speed, threw your son in the air and sped off without attempting to slow or stop. At the very least, the driver is guilty of manslaughter, at worst, murder."

The word hung in the air.

"You do know that our son was potentially part of an inquiry into a very sensitive case of perjury?"

"That is why we had to see you first. To simply ask that you say nothing about your suspicions or anger to anyone. Any word that this is anything other than a tragic accident might drive the culprit or culprits so far underground, our investigation will be hamstrung from the start.

There will be a post mortem and subsequently a coroner's enquiry but they will be more or less routine."

"Will we be allowed to have our son's body back for a funeral?" Cathy Collingham whispered through her tears.

"Once the formalities are over, I cannot see any reason why not."

The two police officers offered more condolences as they said their goodbyes on the front door step.

Chief superintendent Adrian Simpson ushered Charles to one side as his wife crept back into the house.

"I have to tell you, sir, that the real chance of catching the driver is pretty remote. Hit and run accidents happen so quickly very few witnesses have time to react or record what they have seen. The car could have been a Volvo, Mondeo, Nissan or whatever. If this was deliberate and I still have to say IF, we have a mountain to climb to find the murderer, but then," with a tight grin, he continued, "My hobby is mountaineering. Goodnight sir, and may God hold yours and your wife's hands tonight and in the days to come."

Grimly, he settled into the passenger seat as DS Madelaine Coulsdon drove away from the Collingham's house.

"It grieves me to say it, but without Justin's evidence any chance of re-opening the case against Freddie Wharburton has just hit the buffers. If there is a God his way of dealing with evil certainly passeth beyond my understanding."

Chapter 15

"Well, well, well, I will have to ask Gregor for my £25,000 back! This calls for a celebration." Then realising that gloating over a fellow human beings death is a little insensitive, even by his own cynical standards, Gregory resumed, "Well my dear, not of course a celebration, but a sigh of relief that these unfounded accusations against my children are now aborted. I can now again concentrate on the real purpose for my journey of my life, saving Britain!"

If 'Britain' could see you with your trousers around your ankles, banging me against the office door, 'Britain' might think another saviour would be preferable thought Trisha, but simply muttered her agreement.

"Anyway," continued Vlassa, "I have a small errand for you. I am going to be tied up with editorial and cabinet meetings for the next day or so and my lawyer urgently wants to review my will and other private papers to ensure that once I become Prime Minister I am prepared for any eventuality should a nutter wish to shorten my life.

You pompous, self-important egotistical prick, thought Trisha. I should be so lucky to see it happen. But then, as he slipped his arms around her shoulders, she felt the surge of excitement and affection for this extraordinary man weakening her resolve. She did little to resist as he stripped her blouse and bra off, and tore at his flies as she surrendered to her basic primal instincts.

Mopping a mixture of perspiration and semen from her body, Trisha appraised Vlassa with frank amusement.

"So you were saying?"

"Ah yes, my dear. I would be grateful if you would call at my house and collect these papers from the desk in my office there.

Although we may not see eye to eye exactly, my wife Alexandria has the key. Perhaps you could give her a call and let her know you are coming."

"Perhaps I should have done that five minutes ago", Trisha observed tartly.

"Now, now," responded Vlassa, "Sarcasm doesn't suit you, so just get on with it."

It was a very pleasant drive out of London into the Berkshire countryside. Nestled down a country lane between Maidenhead and Henley overlooking the Thames, Vlassa's country house was everything a successful mogul should possess. A long drive from handsome wrought iron gates led to a fine Queen Anne style mansion.

Although she had her memory of having met Alexandria at a reception years before, she was surprised to be greeted warmly at the front door by an attractive, slim and obviously expensively groomed lady in her mid-fifties.

"You must be Trisha, I've heard quite a lot about you from Gregory."

Her eyes twinkled as she said, "He says that without you to organise his life he wouldn't know how to sleep at night, or perhaps he really meant, where to sleep at night."

Trisha stood and looked aghast at this sweet looking, demure lady who, within seconds of her arrival, stripped away any pretence of innocence.

"Don't look so upset my dear," said Alexandria, "Come and have a cup of tea. You aren't the first and I don't suppose you'll be the last. Although that's probably the last thing you want to hear, but you do seem nicer than the rest."

Weakly Trisha was led into a sumptuous drawing room where a tray of tea and cakes had been laid. After they had exchanged a few pleasantries, Alexandria put her cup down and said in a quiet voice

"Just one word of warning, my dear, Gregory is a self-centred bastard which you may have already perceived. He allows nothing to stand in his way. If ever you have cause to reject him, make sure you have some place safe to hide."

"Anyway, I am sure you don't want to hear me rabbiting on, I'll get the key and you can collect the papers. Perhaps Gregory has finally decided to divorce me, so be warned!"

With this admonishment she stood and moving towards the door, looked out of the window onto the forecourt of the house.

"Is that your rather fine car?" queried Alexandria.

"I've never been interested in being a petrol head, as I think you younger generation describe yourselves, but that does look very smart."

Trisha stood beside her at the window and said, "You really are quite a remarkable lady, and I really wish we could be other people so we could meet again, anyway, who knows? But yes, it is a super car, it's a brand new Range Rover Evoque, and yes, I'm a petrol head and I love it. It's the only perk of the job that gives me a real buzz"

"Something you really do share with Gregory then. Has he never told you of his exotic vintage and classic car collection?"

"No never, where is it?"

"It's here, which is why perhaps he's never invited you to see it. Anyway over the past few years he's been too busy to take much interest in it. If you like, whilst I find the key why don't you wander over and take a look, I'm sure he wouldn't mind."

Trisha walked through to the rear of the house and found a hugely impressive barn style building with quite serious security gates. Letting herself in through a side door with the code Alexandria had given her, her breath was taken away by the array of lines of cars under dust covers. Without counting she estimated there were 30-40 cars lined up.

Delicately pulling aside the first dust cover she discovered a mint Austin Healy 3000, and then a 1950's black Citroen saloon, beloved of the French police. Quickly she moved up and down the lines determined that at a later date she would return and ask Alexandria to allow her time to give this magnificent collection her full attention.

Finally looking at her watch she thought one last one, and a fresh dustcover by the rear roller doors caught her eye. Pulling up the cloth she was disappointed to find a rather mundane dark green saloon, but as she moved down the side of the car her heart almost stopped.

Oh dear God, Oh Jesus, oh dear God in heaven. There plain to see were the near side front wing and headlights crumpled and smashed. She stood frozen, transfixed by what she was looking at. This was the car that ran down the young boy who was going to wreck Gregory Vlassa's life.

She felt herself gagging but held back the bile that rose in her throat. Being sick with no way to mop it up would betray a presence that would send the perpetrators running for cover.

Gazing numbly around her she suddenly had the terrifying thought that she was being recorded on CCTV. Surely this priceless collection would be guarded by the most sophisticated equipment money could buy. Surreptitiously looking around however she could see no dark accusing eyes peering at her. Nevertheless, she made a great show of opening her handbag and carelessly dropping her powder compact onto the floor. Realising that time was running out, she quickly emptied the contents of the plastic container back into the bag. Using her nail file she scraped samples of fabric and what she assumed could only be blood and skin from the bodywork and broken glass.

Replacing the cover she returned to the house, Alexandria handed her the key and said,

"You look quite disconcerted, are you okay?"

"I'm okay thank you, a bit breathless from trying to see so many fantastic cars so quickly."

"Well you're welcome to come another time, but here's the key to the desk. Gregory's office is on the first floor down the left hand corridor.

Trisha drove like an automaton back into London, realising her life could never be the same again. The implications were too obvious. Gregory had given Gregor carte blanche to solve his problem for once and for all. And he had.

Trisha kept glancing at the handbag on the seat beside her and realised that it contained material more explosive than nitro glycerine and just as unstable. Who, who, who could she turn to? Finally she realised there was only one person who could be relied upon to take charge, the Telegraph editor Richard Goodfellow. But would even he risk his career, his pension and maybe even his own safety, and that of his family by taking up cudgels against his mendacious and vindictive boss. With the greatest trepidation, Trisha knew there was only one way to find out.

Faced with the most personally challenging confrontation to his journalists integrity, Richard Goodfellow spoke to his secretary and told her he wasn't taken any calls. Lacing his fingers together, he peered at Trisha and said:

"You do have some idea of what we are about to do? From what you have told me, Gregor has a mole in the police, so keeping any initial inquiry secret is going to prove very difficult. However, there may be a route into this that could work. For your own protection I am not going to reveal how it may be achieved. Believe me Trisha, Alexandria's warning about Gregory should never be underestimated."

Three days later the forensic laboratory that Goodfellow had cautiously approached through very confidential friends in the Surrey police where he lived, confirmed through their own contacts in the Suffolk police force that these samples did indeed match those of Justin Collingham's DNA and clothing stored by the hit and run investigators.

Chapter 16

"You never gave a thought when you witnessed Gregory Vlassa handing Gregor £25,000 that there was anything sinister about his motive?"

The Chief Inspector put in charge of the revitalised police team clearly now investigating murder rather than manslaughter, abruptly challenged Trisha Ellson.

"God forgive me, but Gregory Vlassa is, probably was, my boss and was then lover so I closed my mind to what were the potential implications of what, after all could have been the simple offer of a bribe to shut Justin up. You of all people in the police know the adage 'every man has his price'."

Trisha Ellson held back her tears as the frigid response to her declaration revealed little sympathy amongst the group of officers listening to her testimony.

"Okay, okay, thank you Miss Ellson. Get cracking team A with a warrant for Gregor Boroskvy's arrest on suspicion of murder. Team B get a warrant for the impounding of the vehicle stored at Vlassa's home and warrant for his arrest on suspicion of being an accessory to murder. Thirdly, team C bring the twins in for questioning on suspicion of perjury in the case of Freddie Wharburton."

The Chief Commissioner for Scotland Yard who had sat silently listening to the events unfolding, took Richard Goodfellow to one side.

"How long do you plan to hold off publishing any of this story, bearing in mind no one outside this room except maybe our mole, has any inclination of this incredulous crime scenario?"

"Once you have secured the car and arrested Gregor, then I'll publish it. My future with the Telegraph may be history but what a way to go down. The pen mightier than the sword, and all that bollocks. But it isn't bollocks is it? It's actually what the freedom of the press and investigative journalism is all about. Funnily enough not you, not my fellow editors or the jury, who may try this case, are the judge of my conscience. But my wife, who would never forgive me if I capitulated and walked away from a boy and man I've never met, but whose lives never deserved this shit."

Chapter 17

"This is the UK Border Agency in Dover. We have a man attempting to board the Calais P&O ferry with a passport in the name of Gregor Boroskvy. He did not offer any resistance and is currently being held by Dover police. Please confirm that this man is the required suspect in your inquiries."

"I'll kill the bastard who tipped him off," swore Chief Superintendent Adrian Simpson. "Tell whoever is responsible for interviewing Boroskvy that never mind the conspiracy with Vlassa, the name of his grass will give him huge browning points when he comes to trial."

Individually the twins were picked up from their respective private schools and taken to the Suffolk police HQ in Ipswich. They were accompanied by specially selected police officers who were trained to deal with high profile suspects. They were read their rights in front of local solicitors brought in to ensure no legal rights infringements could be insinuated.

Gregory Vlassa was arrested and cautioned as he was about to enter No10 for a cabinet meeting that to all intents and purposes was about to force the PMs resignation and rubber stamp Vlassa's appointment in his place.

The flatbed truck arrived at Vlassa's mansion and winched the green Volvo on board. Alexandria watched dispassionately as the lorry disappeared down the drive.

"Time, I think", she said to no one. "To move on."

"Your call is long overdue my dear," said a sympathetic voice at the end of the phone. "But be assured, you will walk away with every penny you deserve for the years of humiliation this animal has subjected you to."

"You don't have to answer the question," murmured the lady solicitor sat alongside Tania Vlassa in a cold grey cell designed to reduce the human spirit to an almost tacit acceptance of guilt. But they can keep you here until bail can be arranged or refused depending on how the magistrates may accept that your freedom may jeopardise the evidence."

Tania slumped in her chair, her face all at once a study in defiance and defeat.

"It's true, we made it up."

The clock on the wall almost stopped ticking as collectively everyone in the room held their breath.

"Can you please repeat your statement again clearly for the recording."

"We made it up. Mr Wharburton never touched or assaulted us. Toby hated him. I didn't care but once we started it was too late to turn back."

"You mean you allowed this totally innocent man to go to prison for 15 years, without once attempting to halt the fraudulent case against him?"

The defence solicitor leaned over and dejectedly said to Tania:

"You do understand the word fraudulent, do you?"

"I am not a child. At least the school I go to teaches us English properly regardless of where you went."

Those listening to this angry retort were sucked into the aura of superiority that those privileged by money or birth sometimes treat lesser mortals.

The solicitor flushed and said, "I will allow you to charge my client as you think fit. I will not argue a case for bail."

'Stew you little bitch' was all over her face as she gathered her papers together and marched from the interview room.

"Tania Vlassa you are hereby formally charged with perjury against one Frederick Wharburton. You will be remanded in custody until further notice, pending charges against your brother Toby Vlassa being brought."

Next morning the Telegraph front page was dominated by a single headline:

'MEDIA MOGUL CHARGED WITH CONSPIRACY FOR MURDER'

The paper flew off the news stands. All other news channels struggled to get into the story so comprehensive was the Telegraph coverage.

Gregor Boroskvy capitulated without a fight, blaming it all on his boss and his own interpretation of what he was being told to do.

After an initial struggle with his interviewers, Toby Vlassa, faced with his sister's confession, finally conceded that the whole charade against Freddie was concocted, and like Topsy just grew and grew until the roller-coaster they had started was going too fast to get off.

Gregory Vlassa simply blustered and barged his way through his preliminary interviews. He dismissed any idea that the £25,000 given to Gregor was intended to subsidise an act of murder. Bribery yes, murder unthinkable. The fact that Trisha Ellson had witnessed the hand over and the accompanying admonishment 'to fix it and fix it good', was simply evidence that he never once ordered the death of the young lad.

"It will go to trial and with Gregor's finger prints all over the car he will go down for murder, but implicating Gregory Vlassa will be up to the jury to decide," quietly stated Robert Goodfellow.

He sat with Trisha Ellson in a nearby pub nursing their drinks. Looking over her shoulder Trisha almost fearfully asked: "do you think he will come after us?"

"He already has, our redundancy notices are waiting for us back in the office. I'm near retirement so my wife and I are not so worried but you, my dear, must start again. Your affair with Vlassa is not the best CV qualification, but I don't think even he will attempt to touch you."

He stretched back on the pub bench and said, "But your moment of glory is best to come. The Attorney General has within the last hour reviewed the case against Freddie Wharburton and has quashed the entire conviction against him.

I have, however, as a huge favour to myself and the part you and the paper have played in this incredible drama persuaded the Attorney General to let you be the first person to bring the news unofficially, of course, to Freddie in Wandsworth Prison."

Trisha stood and said "You are the best person anyone could wish for as a person and a boss. Don't be so sure Gregory has seen the last of us; my solicitor says we have done nothing to merit firing and redundancy is a non-starter. One thing I am certain is, Alexandria would be honoured and humbled to have the opportunity to meet Freddie with me, and apologise for the apocalyptic misery her family have put him through."

They drove through wet London streets to Wandsworth Prison. At first uncomfortable with their close proximity in Trisha's Evoque, their conversation was stilted, but soon the burgeoning respect each had for each other brought confessions of intimacy about their lives that brought wry laughter, especially when comparing experiences with Gregory Vlassa.

They were ushered into the governor's office whose somewhat gloomy demeanour faded their good humour. Perhaps because its only 9 o'clock in the morning prison governors are lacking in amusing chit chat, or perhaps the pervasive miasma of incarcerated men is enough to hammer anyone's optimism about human nature into the ground

Trisha and Alexandria sat in two typical institutional chairs in front of the governor's desk.

"I was warned late last night that you would be coming so I wanted this morning to be a real surprise for Freddie. Unfortunately, I was away yesterday at a home office meeting with other governors and missed the news that arrived from the Court of Appeal. Freddie had applied for remission of his sentence as he had by now served half of his fifteen year term. Normally with good behaviour, this should have been a formality. Freddie, I have to say has been a model prisoner to the extent that many of us wondered whether he was genuinely guilty as charged. However, that is not for us to debate."

The Governor stood and paced behind his desk. Trisha and Alexandria were already experiencing flutters of alarm and shared glances that underlined their concern.

"Freddie was told yesterday that his appeal had failed. It seems that recent high profile paedophilia cases involving well known political and entertainment figures have hardened the judiciaries attitude to early release of convicted child abusers. I'm sorry to say that Freddie was found in the early hours of this morning in his cell dying from self-inflicted cuts to the arteries on his wrists."

The two girls sat dumbfounded. Whatever retribution would be handed out to Vlassa, Gregor and the twins was now all for nothing.

"However, the governor's bleak expression softened slightly and a tight but nevertheless shadow of a smile touched his lips.

"Freddie, who to many was a failure in life, was yet again a failure in taking it. A very experienced prison warder on his rounds in the early hours, peering through the observation grill in Freddie's door saw him lying at what to him seemed an unnatural angle for Freddie who usually slept flat on his back. Freddie is now recuperating in St George's Hospital, Tooting, and I suggest you proceed with haste to his bedside, where your news will, no doubt, hasten his resolve to live again."

Chapter 18

The young, mousey, lady police officer standing outside the door of Room 7C on the third floor of St Georges Hospital, Tooting, watched warily as the two ladies approached down the corridor. Both looked harassed and apprehensive but since neither looked as though they were 'carrying' she allowed them to move close to her before raising a hand to halt them from moving nearer.

The younger of the two women held out a hand containing a document.

"This is an authorisation from the Governor of Wandsworth Prison allowing us to visit Freddie Wharburton."

The police officer quickly scrutinised the one page letter and said: "you do understand I must check this with my own superior officer.".

There was some delay whilst contact was made between the Met police and Wandsworth prison but finally the constable stood aside and ushered them through the door.

In bed, looking a little like a pink cherub was Freddie, still attached to a few drip lines into his arm, but otherwise looking pretty perky.

They stood together at the foot of the bed whilst Freddie appraised them with a bemused look.

"Ah," he said finally, "so the staff have lied to me. I have died and gone to heaven and you are two beautiful angels come to welcome me.".

The two girls spluttered with laughter and said,

"Sorry Freddie to disappoint you, we are here to bring you back to earth with a bump, and we hope, a very welcome landing."

As they explained their mission, they watched Freddie's face crumple as tears began flowing unashamedly down his cheeks.

"Is it true; is this the end or another wind up?"

But it was Alexandria who made the first move to comfort him.

"Freddie it's true and the moment you are fit enough you are free to go home."

"Yes, home", mused Freddie, "that should be an interesting discovery. Anyway perhaps we should introduce ourselves. I am Freddie Wharburton, one time actor and now ex prison inmate at your service."

Trisha Ellson introduced herself with a mock bow, "One time journalist, and now dragon slayer rescuing incarcerated thespians."

Grinning, "I am Alexandria Vlassa, and one time ..."

Before she could continue Freddie fixed her with a stare and broke in:

"Yes, yes I know who you are. We met quite often in my previous life. You were, I remember, the only one of the family to treat me with kindness and courtesy. But you have lied to me as well, I am actually in hell where, as God is my witness, I will surely meet your husband and children mocking me again."

Alexandria risked rejection as she moved to the bedside and took Freddie's hand.

"Words cannot express the grief and remorse I feel at how you have suffered at the hands of my family. But if there is any forgiveness left in you it will accept that at the time it was a mother's job to protect her children. Anyway their fate is now in the hand of the courts and your hell is over. I am divorcing Gregory as we speak and he is already remanded in jail pending his trial for being an accessory to murder."

"Well, dear pretty lady, you are forgiven, now I need to time to consider my return to the stage. Perhaps if they remake 'Birdman of Alcatraz' I could head the audition queue for the leading role."

Trisha noticed that throughout their exchange the couple continued holding hands and the expression between them suggested an intimacy that transcended the fleeting time they had been in each other's company.

"I'll make you a deal", whispered Alexandria. "If you can bear it, the moment you are out of here, I will take you, us, on the holiday of a lifetime." She smiled coyly as she said "And you can perform for me whenever you like."

Trisha blew the two of them a kiss, and waved a simple goodbye as she tiptoed from the room.

Perhaps, she thought, this is the one stage for Freddie that will never again be the loneliest place in the world.

The End

© Peter J Pritchard
   May 2014